"There's more to you than meets the eye."

His gaze swept over her in an appraising fashion as he added, "And what meets the eye is very appealing."

"Why, thank you, Mr. Aegethos," she said dryly.

"Nicos," he said, his eyes still upon her.

Laura met his stare. After a brief pause she repeated, "Nicos," and received a warm smile that made her even more disturbed. She didn't want to like Nicos Aegethos too much; didn't want to notice the sexy glint of the dark eyes or the masculinity of the long, lean body. There could be no future in loving him, and Laura didn't want to find herself trying to mend a broken heart. She preferred things calm and easy to cope with.

"Live dangerously," Nicos suddenly murmured.

Live dangerously? Laura thought. *Not me, Mr. Aegethos.*

Harlequin Presents edition published November 1981
ISBN 0-373-10466-9

Original hardcover edition published in 1981
by Mills & Boon Limited

CHAPTER ONE

LAURA could feel Henry fuming and fretting beside her, his eye on the traffic lights. They turned orange and he pulsated with impatience. Henry had a mania about punctuality. A taxi swerved too close and made him wince. He was not a reckless driver, making his way cautiously through the heavy clog of London traffic, and he was terrified someone might scratch the smooth paintwork of his new car. He glared at the taxi driver, who glared back, daring him to say a word of protest. Backing down, Henry detached his eyes and glanced at his watch.

'I should have left earlier. I hope we aren't going to be late.'

'Don't worry about it,' said Laura with amused exasperation. Not that there was much point in saying that—Henry enjoyed worrying. It was his life work. She looked up at the blue sky, her eyes dazzled by the summer sun, her skin oddly cold. Oh, no, she thought, not again!

'Are you all right, Laura?' Henry sounded anxious.

'Fine,' she lied, because she was sick of admitting how ill she sometimes felt. For years she had worked all the hours God sent without doing more than complain occasionally: 'I'm getting out of this job. Why should I kill myself for peanuts?' But she had gone on working, stumbling from the wards half blind with fatigue, her head aching, her limbs cramped, too weary to do more than fall into bed and sleep like one of the dead.

Now it had all caught up with her, and she hated the helpless weakness of her own body. She felt she was sliding away, the blood drained from her veins. I am not going to faint, she told herself, sitting up and staring at the booming traffic. I am not going to faint.

'It's the heat, I expect,' Henry said optimistically.

'That's what it is.' The heat, the noise, the pressure of London traffic, that grinding sense of urgency you get in a great city.

Laura closed her eyes and thought of some quiet beach where gulls cried from a distance and the air was fresh with salt.

'You need a long rest,' Henry told her as they halted at some more traffic lights.

It was hard to force up her eyelids, but she made it. 'Henry, I'm sick of being treated as though I was made of glass. A little work won't kill me.'

'Pneumonia is a serious illness,' he pointed out.

'I'm aware of that,' she said drily. 'I've studied illness at close quarters for the last seven years.'

'You're sure you want to take this job?' he persisted, and Laura sighed.

'Certain. I'm much better now. I get stronger every day. What I need now is something to keep me occupied. I'm not the type who can sit around doing nothing all day. I'd go out of my mind!'

Henry looked approving. 'I'm sure you're right.'

He was a big man, broad-shouldered and tall, his brown hair flecked with grey, his features oddly youthful. Laura often thought it was his life style which gave Henry that young look. His life was a blank page on which, so far, the years had written very little.

He lived with his mother, a tiny, iron-willed lady who ran his life ruthlessly and meant to choose her own daughter-in-law. Laura wasn't on her list. Mrs Stamford had made that clear the first day they met. Laura had made it clear in turn that she had no such ambition. Henry was a darling, but he wasn't the stuff dreams are made of. Once that problem was out of the way, Mrs Stamford became quite friendly. Of all this, though, Henry was blissfully ignorant. The brief war had gone on over his head. In fact, he often told Laura how glad he was that she got on so well with his mother.

Easing the car forward, he shot a look sideways and said: 'I'm sure you were right to wear your uniform. It makes you look . . .'

'Sensible?' interrupted Laura, tongue in cheek.

'Capable,' he said, and she wondered if that was an improvement on sensible, but decided it wasn't.

When Laura began to recover from her long bout of illness she had been shaken to be told that the hospital felt she should not return to the wards for at least six months.

'You're not up to it,' her physician had said bluntly. 'Take a light job somewhere. Go abroad. Get a few months in the country, if you can. Do anything you like, but keep out of hospital wards until you're back to normal.'

Talking about it to Henry, she had been torn between irritation and misery. She was a dedicated nurse. She didn't want to accept the advice she had been given.

'You must be sensible,' Henry had told her, then he had looked thoughtful. 'I suppose you wouldn't mind leaving the country?'

Laura had begun to laugh. 'Getting rid of me, Henry?'

You couldn't tease him, he took it too seriously. 'Good God, no,' he had protested. 'It was an idea I'd had. One of my clients is looking for a level-headed girl to take charge of her granddaughter.'

'I'm not a children's nurse, Henry.'

An expression of distaste had crossed his face. 'She isn't a child,' he had added with a little shudder. After a pause he had said: 'Far from it.'

Looking interested, Laura had asked: 'How old is she?'

'Sixteen.' For some reason Laura got the feeling Henry was trying not to say too much about the girl. Hurriedly he had gone on: 'Mrs Grey is going abroad and taking the girl with her, but she feels she can't cope with her without help. What she wants is someone young enough to be able to make friends with Amanda, but old enough to be responsible for her.'

'A sort of chaperone?'

Henry nodded happily. 'Exactly. It wouldn't be too tiring for you, Laura. You would be travelling at times, of course, but in the very best of style.'

'They're rich?' Henry's clients often were. He liked them rich. He had a romantic streak that adored the idea of money, and he was a terrific name-dropper. He enjoyed having clients who were household names. It made him feel sophisticated, a man of the world, which was in fact the very opposite of what he was, but Laura looked at him with indulgence as his eyes gleamed happily. Henry really was a sweet man.

'My client is Vanessa Grey,' he had told her, and she had frowned thoughtfully.

'Vanessa Grey?' She knew she had heard the name. It definitely rang a bell. But she was not sure where she had heard it before.

Henry had looked shocked. 'Her husband is Barnaby Grey.'

'The sausage king?'

Looking down his nose, Henry had corrected her, his expression almost shocked. 'His firm does manufacture sausages, among other things.' Henry did not like the description of Mr Grey, however. It was not dignified.

'The papers call him the sausage king.'

'You read the wrong newspapers,' Henry had complained, then he had added: 'But he isn't my client. It's his wife who's on my books, and she's a charming woman.'

Laura had looked at him with amusement. 'Is she?' Henry was very susceptible to female charm, particularly in older women, and when the charm came allied to fame or money Henry was bowled over.

He had beamed. 'Quite charming,' he had insisted.

Curious, Laura had asked: 'How old is she?'

'I'm not sure. Around seventy, I think,' said Henry, altering the picture which had begun to form in Laura's mind of some femme fatale who had bowled him over on sight.

'Shall I arrange for you to meet her?' he had asked, and Laura, after a moment's hesitation, had agreed.

'I think you might be just the sort of girl she is looking for,' he had told her and Laura hadn't known whether to be horrified or flattered.

She was a slender, fine-boned girl with blonde hair which she wore brushed into two smooth wings around her face. Her bone structure and colouring gave her an outward delicacy which disguised the strength of her character. Henry took that look of fragile femininity for the whole woman. He would have been shocked if Laura had told him that she was a lot tougher than he imagined. Henry liked frail girls.

His blindness to her real nature didn't matter. Henry had made no demands on her that she wasn't prepared to concede. The nearest they had got to romance was sharing a box of paper tissues while they watched a sad movie.

Henry was the brother Laura had never had. She wasn't sure what she meant to him, but, despite his heavy gallantry, she suspected she was the sister Henry had never had.

Mrs Grey was currently occupying a large suite in a hotel overlooking one of London's royal parks. Henry left his car with the doorman and ushered

Laura into a lift, his brow creased with anxiety as he looked at his watch. 'We're five minutes late.'

'Relax!' Laura told him.

When they left the lift, a deep carpet received their footsteps soundlessly. The corridor was walled in gilt-edged mirrors which threw back a fractured reflection as they passed. Laura saw her own face, a waxen shade of white, her uniform stressing her pallor. If Mrs Grey had any sense she would reject her at once as a suitable companion for a lively sixteen-year-old.

I look like a walking corpse, Laura thought angrily, and her irritation with herself brought a sweep of colour into her face.

The door was opened after a long interval, and Henry's rigid expression told Laura that the girl who had opened it was the famous Amanda.

She was in plum silk harem trousers tied at the ankle with gold cords, one of which had come undone and trailed after her.

'You'll trip over that,' Laura pointed out with a smile.

Amanda looked furious, but she bent down and tied the cord with a little jerk. Her long black hair fanned out to hide her face, but Laura had already seen enough to have qualms about this job.

'We have an appointment with Mrs Grey,' Henry said in a nervous, pompous voice.

'She'll be here in a minute,' said the girl, straightening. She put her hands on her hips and stared at Laura, who stared back.

Amanda had almond-shaped eyes with long lashes and had outlined them in depth with a brown eyeliner which shaded away to nothing but which gave her gaze a mournful, oddly defensive shadow.

Henry bore her scrutiny uneasily, shifting from one foot to another under it and looking more like a baby elephant than ever, to Laura's amusement.

The girl appeared to have nothing to say, but her dark eyes said it with such biting dislike that Laura felt like walking out of the suite without waiting to meet Mrs Grey.

Glancing down, she saw the girl's hands clenched at her sides and noticed that they were trembling slightly. Not so cool, after all, she thought, quickly looking up and meeting the dark eyes before Amanda had a chance to shield them and their expression. No, Laura thought, not as cool as she would like me to think.

A door opened and a vision rushed into the room at breakneck speed. For an instant Laura could not believe that this was the old lady she had been brought here to meet, then Henry stepped forward, his worried face breaking into a beam, his hand held out. 'Mrs Grey, how nice to see you again!'

'So sorry to keep you waiting, Henry, I was on the telephone and I couldn't get away, try as I might. This is so good of you, isn't it, Mandy? Very thoughtful to go to all this trouble just for us, and we do appreciate it.' All the time she was talking to Henry her little black eyes were flicking to Laura and away again, taking in every detail, the slant of them exactly like that of her granddaughter, the shape and proportion of her face similar too. Her hair was styled in a youthful fashion which gave her silvery hair an odd look of being artificial, as though she had had it dyed that shade. Her youthful mask startled at first sight, but her eyes had the clever, sad knowledge of experience.

She had the slim upright figure of a much younger woman, her movements light and graceful, her wrists elegant as she gestured with ringed hands.

Laura felt that, much against her first judgment on sight, she was going to like her. Those eyes drew one, made a silent apology for the brittle falsity of her appearance, held wry self-mockery and a sad appeal.

Henry was mumbling an introduction and Mrs Grey moved to shake hands. She held Laura's hand while she studied her face. 'Yes, I can see you've been ill. Are you sure you're better? Well enough to take a trip abroad?'

Laura hesitated, smiling. 'I think so. I do still get tired at odd moments, but every day it gets easier.'

'We won't be going for a week,' Mrs Grey told her. 'Pneumonia, Henry said?'

'Yes. It came at a bad time. I'd been working rather hard.' Laura smiled again and the sad, dark eyes smiled back.

'Come and sit down and we'll have some coffee. Mandy will ring for it.' Mrs Grey led Laura to a couch on the far side of the room. The sunshine fell in a light stream over blue leather and grey silk brocade, picked out the pale blue flowers in the patterned carpet. Henry came behind them and sat down in a chair nearby, his hands on his knees, to gaze at them with avuncular satisfaction. Laura glanced at him with affectionate wryness. He was pleased with himself because he thought his scheme was going to work.

Mandy was talking on the telephone. She came back, her hand thrusting back the full black hair in a sulky gesture. 'Be up in a minute.'

Her grandmother gave her a hopeful smile. 'Why don't you go and change, dear? You won't want to go out to lunch in those.'

'Yes, I will.' Mandy had the air of one who makes no concessions. She shifted her gum around her mouth, watching her grandmother like a cat watching a mouse. Laura got the distinct impression that Amanda enjoyed playing games with her elders, defying them until they were forced to positive action. She could remember the feeling. In happy children it is a way of establishing boundaries, trying out the limits of their own personal territory and power. In unhappy children it is a form of rebellion and an act of revenge.

Mrs Grey turned to Laura. 'She really can't have lunch wearing them, can she?'

Laura looked at the harem trousers. 'Oh, everyone's wearing them at the moment, Mrs Grey, although it's just as well Amanda's so slim, because they do tend to make you look a bit like a panto horse.'

Amanda gave her a killing look and vanished. Mrs Grey put a hand over her mouth like a schoolgirl, giggling. Henry laughed in sympathy, although not quite sure what the joke was.

'She's at the difficult stage,' Mrs Grey said, glancing over her shoulder to make sure the door was closed and Amanda not in earshot. She lowered her tone, closing a hand over Laura's in a tight grip. 'We've had a good deal of trouble from her lately. It's always hard for a motherless child, I suppose. She's growing up too fast and the schools don't seem to know how to cope with her.'

'A firm hand,' Henry proffered. 'That's what she needs.' There was little doubt that he had not taken to Amanda. He was both uneasy and irritated in her presence. Henry had picked up that contemptuous mockery in her stare and he had not liked it.

Mrs Grey smiled on him, but her dark eyes held a spark of disagreement. She had a way of not saying what was in her mind which suggested to Laura that she was used to dealing with difficult men. Laura had learnt to do that, herself. In the wards a doctor's decision was final even if a nurse was absolutely certain he was wrong. Laura had learnt to convey her disagreement without saying a syllable. She recognised the technique.

'Have you any other grandchildren?' she asked, and Mrs Grey switched her glance to her.

'No, she's the only one. My son shows no signs of giving me any more, either.' She sounded rather sad about that, but she smiled again, meeting Laura's eyes.

'And Amanda has been at boarding school?'

'She started going away to school when she was eight.' Catching Laura's expression, Mrs Grey sighed. 'Yes, I think it was too young, too, but her father insisted. He thought the discipline would be good for her.'

Oh, he was that sort of father, was he? Laura looked sideways and saw Henry nodding vigorously in approval.

'She got in with rather a wild set at her last school. We were relieved to get her away from them.'

'She's sixteen?' Laura asked, and Mrs Grey nodded.

'I can't keep up with her,' Mrs Grey murmured with a sigh. 'She makes me feel old.'

At seventy that wasn't so surprising, but it was difficult to believe that Mrs Grey was anywhere near that age. She wasn't so much well-preserved as impossible to place—apart from her eyes, her face had a carefully constructed plasticity which was deceptive at a distance.

Henry protested at once. 'Good heavens, you aren't . . .' Words failed him, but his expression was sincere enough to get another smile out of Mrs Grey. That heavy schoolboy admiration was endearing. She liked Henry.

'They expel her,' she told Laura, looking at her sadly. 'She never seems to settle at any of them.'

Laura could guess why. Amanda had that rebellious eye. No doubt she had learnt to manipulate the adults around her from an early age. It would be one way of ensuring a constant stream of attention.

'It's a difficult age,' said Laura.

'Laura's used to keeping young girls in line,' Henry told Mrs Grey, and got a reproachful look that made him shift uneasily in his chair.

'What Amanda needs is someone who will understand her,' Mrs Grey said to him, but with an eye on Laura.

'Of course,' Henry agreed hurriedly.

'You're going to Europe, I gather,' said Laura, to divert attention from his uneasy writhing. Poor Henry, he only wanted to please. It wasn't his fault if he kept putting his foot in it.

'Yes, first to Paris, to buy some clothes, then on to Italy or maybe Greece. Amanda hasn't seen her father for some time and she should spend some time with him. He spends some weeks in Greece every summer.'

Did that idea appeal to him? wondered Laura. She had heard very little about Amanda's father apart from the fact that he was Mrs Grey's only child, the product of her first marriage, to a Greek shipping magnate.

'He's very busy,' Mrs Grey murmured plaintively. 'He doesn't really have the time for her that he would like.'

Their eyes met. Laura read the reluctant admission in the dark eyes. Domenicos Aegethos wasn't a family man by nature and his life wasn't organised in a way that left much room for his daughter.

'Her mother died recently?'

'When Amanda was four. I took her into my care after that until she went to school.' Mrs Grey obviously did not want to go into all that. She looked vaguely at Laura's uniform. 'You don't have to wear that, do you? I hate anything that reminds me of hospitals.'

'As you like,' Laura promised. She had worn her

uniform to project the right image. Henry might see her as a frail little woman, but Laura knew that her uniform was a better guide to her character.

Mrs Grey looked relieved. 'Tell me more about yourself, my dear.'

'What do you want to know?' Laura had never been interviewed for a job before. She had worked in the hospital since she was eighteen and her life had been entirely bounded by the hospital walls.

'What made you go into nursing?'

Laura smiled politely. 'I liked the idea of being a nurse, I suppose,' she told the older woman evasively. Her dedication was deeper than she had any intention of admitting. Her parents had been killed in a car crash when she was fifteen. Laura had been in the back of the car and had escaped with minor injuries, but her mother had died in her arms on the roadside. Laura had never forgotten her own sense of helpless misery. She had felt that if she only knew what to do she might stop her mother dying, and the experience had left her with an indelible desire to be a nurse.

Although Laura had a strong sense of humour, her nature was deeply serious. She had had to hide her amusement in the wards so often it had become second nature to her to look cool and remote. The blonde delicacy of her looks had helped. In her uniform she looked as if she never smiled in her life.

Her dedication to her career had left little time for romance. When she staggered off duty she was often so tired that a warm bath and an early night was more appealing than a date with a member of the opposite sex.

'The only use I have for a bed tonight is to sleep in it,' she had once told one of the young doctors, shutting him out of her flat with a firm smile.

'You don't know what you're missing,' he had hissed through the keyhole.

'Tell me in the morning,' she had yawned.

'Have a heart, Laura!'

'I've got one, thanks, and it's working just fine,' she had said as she walked away.

Her illness had taken her by surprise. Her concentration on her job had been so intense that it had never occurred to her to question her own state of health. When a dose of 'flu had turned without warning into pneumonia, her physician had given her a scolding, if kindly, lecture on overworking.

'You're a very silly girl,' he had told her.

'I'm sorry,' Laura had said, smiling at him with affection, because he had probably saved her life during the crisis of the illness. Her own strength hadn't been enough to pull her through. It had taken the combined determination of the whole medical staff to do it.

Mrs Grey was talking about Amanda when Laura surfaced again from her rueful memories of the past.

'Do you think you could manage her?'

'I could try,' Laura said doubtfully. Amanda looked sulky and difficult, but she didn't look impossible.

'All I want you to do is keep her out of trouble,' Mrs Grey added with a long, deep sigh. 'I won't pretend she's easy to deal with, but I'm very fond of

her. I'm hoping to persuade her father to join us now
and then. He may be too busy, but he may find time
to come, especially when he hears that there'll be
someone looking after Amanda and keeping her out
of his hair.'

Poor Amanda, thought Laura, watching a pigeon
which had landed on the windowsill outside and was
strutting and cooing as it paraded along the wide
window. Clearly nobody wanted Amanda around.
She had been shunted off to a boarding school at an
age when she was too young, and had, quite
naturally, rebelled against an institutionalised exist-
ence in every way she could. Far from bringing her
family to a realisation of her unhappiness, it had
merely made them annoyed with her and reluctant
to put up with her.

Mrs Grey had been watching her and now she
said defensively: 'We're neither of us young people.
Amanda's not easy to deal with, her schools find her
quite a handful. They can't manage her, so how
could Barny and I hope to?'

Laura gave her a smile, probing her face and
seeing the wariness of defeat in her eyes. Mrs Grey
wasn't blind to Amanda's problems at all. She knew
her granddaughter was unhappy, but perhaps she
felt genuinely that she was too old to do anything
about it. It was not easy to read her true character
from that smooth, unreal mask. Only the sad dark
eyes betrayed a thing. Life had left marks on Mrs
Grey in the past and although she had covered them
up, smothered them with plastic surgery and cos-
metics, her eyes were a dead giveaway. All her money

couldn't buy her contentment, and, despite her lively manner and the sophisticated glitter of jewellery and expensive clothes, Mrs Grey was not a contented woman.

Henry was making mumbled noises of agreement, leaning forward, his face soothing. Laura glanced at him and got an agonised look. Henry was disturbed by the course of the conversation. He had picked up Laura's silent criticism and was alarmed by it.

Laura looked back at Mrs Grey. 'Your son couldn't . . .' she began, and Mrs Grey interrupted with a light laugh and a nervous flash of those sad eyes.

'Domenicos is always so busy. He carries a great burden on his shoulders.'

The door opened and Amanda sauntered into the room. She had changed out of the offending trousers and was now wearing a little cream suit with a blouson top. Her grandmother looked at her with relief and approval. Amanda ignored her, staring rudely at Laura, as though daring her to smile.

Taking a posed position at the window, an elbow propping her dark head, she gazed out across the tree-etched London skyline like a sailor scanning wide horizons. It was an elegant little picture and meant to be admired. Amanda was drawing attention to herself. Was that what she always wanted? Were all her rebellions and alarums meant to force the indifferent adults in her life to focus their attention on her, however reclutantly?

'Mandy, Miss Crawford . . . no, I can't call you that all the time! May I call you Laura?' Mrs Grey smiled at her and Laura smiled back, nodding.

'Mandy, Laura has decided to come with us,' Mrs Grey told the back of Amanda's head.

'Oh, great,' Amanda drawled without bothering to turn round, and Mrs Grey looked helplessly at Laura, apology in her face.

Laura smiled back at her, getting up, and Mrs Grey rose too, offering her hand.

'It was very nice to meet you. I'm sure you and Amanda are going to get on well together.' She shot a doubtful look at the back of the silent girl at the window, opening her mouth to speak again, but as she did so the door opened and a man walked into the room.

Mrs Grey glanced round in surprise and gasped, putting a hand to her throat in shock.

'Domenicos!'

Amanda spun, stiffening, the dark slant of her eyes all pupil as she stared across the room at the new arrival.

'Surprised to see me?' He had a deep, cool voice which held an ironic note, and he didn't even glance at the two strangers in the room, as though their presence didn't impinge upon his consciousness.

'Why didn't you let me know you were coming to London? What are you doing here? I thought you were in New York or Athens.' Mrs Grey moved towards him. He bent and brushed his lips lightly and distantly across her cheek before straightening again.

'I'm here on business,' he said, then looked at his daughter. 'Hallo, Amanda.'

She came forward, her lower lip held in a sulky

little pout, and offered him her cheek with unhidden reluctance.

Laura watched, probing his face with a thoughtful eye. She had realised who he was the moment he walked into the room, of course, but she would never have recognised him from the few photographs she had seen of him in newspapers. He was better looking than she had expected. The grey reproduction of newsprint could not do justice to his colouring, or give you any hint of the immediate impact of his physical presence. He was a tall, lean man with a way of walking that spoke of restless impatience, his tanned skin taut over his hard, angular cheekbones. His voice had a definite foreign intonation in some words, but he used English fluently and without a sign of hesitation.

'You've changed,' he told Amanda, looking her up and down, and the girl's skin glowed with colour.

'What did you expect? Thought you'd see me in a gym-suit, did you?'

His brows met above those dark eyes. 'Are you well?' he asked, impatience in his face, and Laura was struck by the odd stiffness of the way he talked to his own daughter, as though she was a stranger. Perhaps she was? Perhaps Domenicos Aegethos hardly knew his own child.

Amanda wasn't bothering to disguise her resentment and hostility towards him any more than she had bothered with Laura. 'Why would you care?' she asked him. 'It's months since I saw you.'

'I'm very busy, you know,' he said shortly.

'You always are!'

'I have a great many responsibilities,' he said, pushing his hands into his pockets and looking at her with that impatience. His profile had the hard clarity of a face on a coin; his nose straight and chiselled, his black hair thick and glossy. It was an impressive face but it wasn't the face of a man who was likely to be indulgent with other people's weaknesses. The strong austere planes of his face suggested that he was far from indulgent with his own. The only indication of sensuality came in the full lower lip which, even when it wasn't smiling, had a distinct warmth in the curve of it.

Laura was struck by a faint resemblance between him and his daughter. Amanda's face was that of a young girl, her unformed character in the lines of cheek and jaw, but a nagging likeness showed between them as the two of them stared at each other. Amanda was obstinate. Was that what she had inherited from her father?

'I didn't realise you were with your grandmother at the moment,' he said, his voice carrying the hint of an effort to placate Amanda.

It failed. Amanda glared at him. 'You hardly know I'm alive at all, why should you know where I am or what I'm doing?'

He drew an audible breath, his body held in visible tension. 'Don't speak to me like that!'

Amanda gave one of her insolent little shrugs. Her father turned to speak to his mother, and caught sight of Laura and Henry. His eyes flashed angrily over them, his face bearing dark red betrayal of temper, and Laura watched coolly as his straight black brows drew together as he realised that his meeting with his family had been observed by strangers.

Mrs Grey waved a hand towards Laura and Henry. 'Nicos, this is my lawyer, Henry Stamford, and that's Laura Crawford who's coming to Europe with us.'

'Europe with you?' Domenicos Aegethos repeated that in a curt tone. He flicked his eyes over Laura and looked back at his mother. 'Europe? When is this? Why isn't Amanda at school?'

'Well——' hesitated his mother.

'I got the boot,' Amanda said bluntly.

He swung his black head back towards her with a dangerous expression on his face. 'What did you say?'

'I was slung out, packed off, expelled,' Amanda recited with an unhidden enjoyment.

'What?' The roar was throttled after that first word. Domenicos Aegethos tautened and turned to face the two standing at the door. 'Will you kindly excuse us?' he asked before striding over to wave them out of the suite. The door slammed behind him.

As they moved away Laura heard the rush of deep, angry words and said under her breath: 'Whew! . . . that's what's called hitting the roof. Why didn't they tell him? Or do they prefer to keep him in the dark?'

'Oh, dear,' Henry groaned, almost wringing his hands, 'how very unfortunate!'

'You can say that again! He looked livid. If this is around the dozen mark, Amanda has put the tin lid on her previous efforts, I'd say.'

'It isn't funny, Laura,' Henry chided. 'Poor Mrs Grey, I know she was dreading telling her son. He has an explosive temper, it seems.'

'It does seem,' Laura agreed. They were waiting for the lift, but even at the end of a corridor she could still hear that brusque, deep voice and his flow of language seemed unstoppable. 'But I would say poor Amanda, myself.'

'She hasn't behaved very well,' Henry agreed, without real sympathy.

'If you keep a cat in a cage you must expect it to try to escape,' Laura murmured.

'Don't be absurd, Laura. A good English boarding school can't be described as a cage.'

'If you ask me, from what I've seen and been told, the whole of that girl's life has been a cage,' said Laura as she stepped into the lift.

CHAPTER TWO

'Can I give you lunch?' Henry asked as they drove away, and Laura shook her head.

'I've a lot to do, thanks,' she smiled. 'So have you, I'm sure.'

He didn't deny it. He had a crowded schedule, his practice not large, but exclusive. Henry liked his clients to be out of the top drawer. He found the lives of people like Domenicos Aegethos glamorous and liked moving on the fringe of that world.

'Do you think you can cope with that girl?' he asked as he stopped his car outside her flat.

'I've no idea, but it would be fun to try.'

'She's impossible,' said Henry, frowning.

'She's unhappy,' Laura said gently, as she got out of the car. Her flatmate, Beth, wouldn't be home yet and Laura could have a quiet afternoon without needing to talk to anyone. She still found it tiring to be with people. Beth was a darling, but she was very exhausting. 'I'll see you, Henry,' she added, smiling at him.

She got herself a light lunch and was resting on her bed, reading, when the phone rang. Laura answered absently.

'Miss Crawford?' The deep timbre of the voice was unmistakable and her heart sank. He was going to tell her she hadn't got the job.

'Yes,' she said with a sigh.

'Aegethos,' he announced, quite unnecessarily.

'Oh, hallo,' said Laura in a bright voice and could have kicked herself for sounding like a fool.

'Miss Crawford, I think you and I should have a talk,' he informed her. 'Can you come over to my London offices?'

'Now?' Laura asked. Yes, she thought. He's going to tell me I'm not going to Europe. Oh, well, it was a nice thought.

'Now,' he said curtly.

'Where . . .' she began, and he broke in with a brusque tone.

'Take a taxi. Tell the driver you want the Worldwide Trust building, Dryden Square.'

'Dryden——,' Laura started to repeat when the click of the phone told her she had been cut off. The phone whirred at her and she made a face at it before she hung up.

Her skirt was slightly crumpled where she had been lying on the bed. She had got into the habit of resting at frequent intervals during her convalescence after she was released from the hospital. At first it had irked her to recognise how quickly her stupid body could tire of such mundane tasks as shopping or housework, but she had been forced, by a grey exhaustion when she ignored her own condition, to come to terms with the way things were for the moment. Mr Mackenzie had assured her that gradually everything would return to normal. 'It takes time,' he had said. 'And you overdid things in the past, so now you're paying for it.'

Laura monitored her own state whenever she

remembered to do so, and she knew he was right. Every day she had to rest less and she felt stronger, but she knew it would take a little more time.

She hesitated over her uniform for a moment, then decided not to wear it. She chose instead a simple brown linen suit which gave an impression of cool formality. The cream silk blouse she wore under it was sufficient to soften it and she was satisfied with her colour this afternoon. Her rest and the surprise of Domenicos Aegethos's phone call had put a faint pink into her face. Brushing her blonde hair until it fell into those two smooth wings, she decided she looked better than she had done recently.

As instructed, she took a taxi and the driver made his way through heavy London traffic to Dryden Square. It was behind Oxford Street, she discovered, not far from Marble Arch, and she saw the Worldwide Trust building before they reached it, the greenish stone and great rows of windows visible above the roofline as they weaved their way towards it.

'One of them new blocks,' the driver commented as he spluttered into the curb, his engine coughing before it cut out.

Laura climbed out and looked up at the towering building. 'Was it built recently? I don't remember seeing it before.'

'Couple of years,' the driver guessed, leaning on his lowered window. He looked at the meter and told her the fare. Having paid it, Laura walked into the block, through smoked glass swing doors which gave a cool interior to the cream marble foyer. It looked more like the entrance to a luxury hotel than an office block. Great cream stone urns held spilling plants and on the walls hung modernistic prints in stark colours. At a wide polished desk sat a girl in a sleek black dress who smiled at Laura invitingly as she paused to look around. 'Can I help you?'

'I'm here to see Mr Aegethos,' said Laura, and saw the girl's eyes flicker before she smiled again in a very different way.

'Is he expecting you?'

'Yes,' Laura said.

'Would you sit down, please? Could I have your name?'

Laura sat down on a comfortable, deep-upholstered chair, giving her name. The girl lifted a phone and spoke softly while Laura looked up at the open, echoing ceiling through which the wide flight of stairs passed to a higher floor. Across the foyer a row of lifts were in constant operation, the doors sliding open and shut smoothly. People came and went, talking, giving Laura sideways looks from time to time but usually intent on their conversations.

'Someone will come down for you,' the girl told Laura as she turned back to her with an even warmer smile. She arranged the leather-framed blotter on her desk into a perfect rectangle and inspected Laura discreetly under lowered lashes.

Dying to ask me questions, Laura thought. But too well trained to do anything of the kind. Looking up at a picture behind the girl's head Laura followed the intricate swirl of black and red, wondering what it was meant to represent. It looked interesting, anyway, but the tiny dots of colour might end up by giving you migraine if you looked at it too hard.

'Miss Crawford?'

Absorbed in the picture, she had not noticed the arrival of the man bending beside her. She rose, startled, and he gave her a beneficent smile. Tall, thin, stooped, he had a bald head rising out of thin black hair and his face was a neutral territory into which his thoughts never ventured.

'This way, please,' he intoned, waving her towards the side of the foyer farthest from the row of lifts. Laura followed him down a side corridor and stopped at another lift, standing open. The man gestured for her to enter and joined her. The door slid shut and the lift rose silently.

'I'm George Ryan, Mr Aegethos's personal assistant,' the man introduced himself with a faint smile.

'Oh,' Laura achieved, wondering whether to express sympathy or look impressed. In the end she did neither, merely nodded.

He was a man in his late forties or early fifties. He dressed extremely well, but in a style intended, she suspected, to merge into his background and make him invisible. A sort of Savile Row camouflage? She got the impression of someone hidden, hard to know. His voice was soft and unstressed, his movements smooth to the point of being stealthy.

Perhaps that was what Domenicos Aegethos paid him for—that discreet and silent withdrawal into cover? She wondered how important he was and why it had been he who had come down to meet her and escort her to the royal presence. Or had it been his own decision to do it? Had Aegethos merely barked: 'Get her,' and George Ryan decided to do it himself so that he could take a good look at her?

While she had been inspecting him he had been giving her the same treatment. The constant surveillance of his pale blue eyes made her feel like someone being X-rayed.

'Beautiful weather,' he remarked.

'Lovely.'

'Do you live in London, Miss Crawford?'

'Fulham,' Laura told him.

'Really?' He sounded as though not quite sure where that was, his brows curving up slightly. 'You're a staff nurse at St Aidan's?'

'Yes,' she admitted. Was that intended to show her that he knew all about her or was he merely making conversation?

She mistook him. He gave her an almost human smile. 'I once had an ingrown toenail treated there.'

Laura laughed. 'Very painful.'

'They are, aren't they?' His blue eyes took on a spark of liveliness. 'I became quite obsessed with the toe. Strange how such little things can take over your mind for days at a time.'

'Pain does that.' She had seen so many people in pain and had grown to recognise the inward-turning look of someone fighting with it.

Having established a form of kinship with him she ventued to ask: 'Is this Mr Aegethos's private lift?'

'Oh, yes,' he said, as though that had to be obvious, and of course it was, she had guessed at once from its splendid isolation down that corridor. The amazing Mr Aegethos wasn't sharing lifts with any of his employees.

The lift had stopped and the door slid open. Laura walked out into a wide, pale blue corridor lit with sunlight streaming from a great picture window to the left. Mr Ryan ushered her with a wave towards a door. His knock was answered by a muffled: 'Come.'

Opening the door for her, Mr Ryan announced: 'Miss Crawford, sir.' He stood back and Laura passed him. Her eye fell on Domenicos Aegethos at once. He sat to one side of the room, behind a desk, and behind his black head hung a large portrait of a man who might have been the man at the desk if the background and the man's clothes had not somehow made it plain that this was someone else. His father? Laura wondered as she walked towards him, her eye flicking from the living to the painted face and trying to decide on the relationship.

The living man leaned back with his head against the padded leather of the chair, swivelling slightly, studying her with his black eyes half sheathed by their heavy lids. Sunlight carved shadows on his cheeks, gave a deeper gloss to the thick black hair.

His fingers tapped on the underside of his desk. 'Sit down, please,' he murmured, and she got the feeling he had added the final word as an after-thought.

Laura sat, facing him, her hands demurely in her lap like a schoolgirl before the headmistress.

'How much has my mother told you about my daughter's recent behaviour?'

The abrupt question left Laura speechless for a

moment. After gathering her thoughts together she admitted: 'Very little. I know she's been expelled from her school and that she's difficult.'

'Difficult?' He repeated the word with a wry twist of his mouth, his eyes cynical. 'Yes, that's one way of describing it, I suppose.'

'How would you describe it?'

He drew in his lower lip for a second before releasing it, giving a little shrug. 'Let's just say that before you decide whether you feel adequate to the task of shadowing Amanda around half Europe, I think you should have a slightly clearer idea of just what Amanda's notion of being difficult is . . .' He paused to consider her, as if watching her reaction, and Laura nodded.

'I see.' That sounded very reasonable, and it certainly was not the out-and-out dismissal she had been half expecting.

'My mother told you she was expelled from her last school?' he asked.

Nodding, Laura agreed.

'Did she tell you why?'

She shook her head and saw his mouth give that wry little twist again.

'I had a feeling she might not have done,' he said. 'She was expelled after staying out all night at a party for which she had not had permission.'

That didn't sound so very terrible, thought Laura. Naughty, perhaps, but surely not quite unforgivable.

The dark eyes pierced her face and he smiled grimly, shaking his head.

'No, that's not it,' he said with dry emphasis.

'When she came back in the morning she was in what they politely described to me as "an excited state".' He looked directly at Laura, the heavy-lidded eyes glittering. 'She'd been taking drugs.'

'Oh, dear!' Laura exclaimed, horrified.

'My mother didn't tell you that?'

'She certainly didn't,' said Laura, frowning. That altered the whole picture. 'Was it the first time?'

'That isn't quite clear,' he told her. 'I asked that myself, of course. Amanda claims it was, but God knows how far you can believe her.'

'What had she been taking?'

He shrugged his wide shoulders, tilting back his head against his chair. 'Hard to say. I don't think she knows herself. The school called a doctor, of course, but at the time Amanda was too high to give any convincing answer, and afterwards she said she couldn't remember.'

Laura's brows knit together, her eyes disturbed. 'You've discussed this with her?'

'Oh, yes,' he said, and the grim tone made Laura very sorry for Amanda. 'I've also been on the phone to the school. They couldn't tell me much more than I'd got from Amanda, though.'

'I suppose it was some sort of gesture,' Laura said reflectively, trying to fit the new information about Amanda into what she already knew, and Domenicos Aegethos leaned forward angrily, his eyes flashing.

'Don't ever let her hear you talk like that! I don't want her to think we're going to excuse this away.'

'I wasn't excusing anything,' Laura retorted, returning his glare with interest. 'I'm just trying to understand her.'

'You're not required to understand her. You're being employed to watch her like a hawk and keep her out of any more trouble!'

'Don't you think it might help if I understood what made her tick?' Laura asked with a trace of sarcasm, and he stiffened in his chair, his dark eyes narrowing to a hard sheen. The strong lines of his face took on an uncompromising fixity, and there was no warmth whatever in that hard, straight mouth.

'I can tell you what makes Amanda tick,' he said tersely. 'She gets a kick out of causing trouble.'

'I wonder why that is,' Laura murmured, her wide blue eyes holding his stare.

His mouth tightened. 'She's a female,' he said with biting cynicism.

Laura's brows rose at his tone, the barbed hostility of the curt words.

'What Amanda needs isn't understanding,' he told her, 'it's discipline. If I had time I'd see to it myself, but I don't have time to spare at the moment. I wanted to see you to make sure you knew what the situation was. Do you think you can be tough with her?'

Laura didn't answer, but her wide blue eyes spoke for her, and the man opposite had no difficulty in deciphering their expression.

'You don't know anything about us, Miss Crawford,' he told her, a hint of impatience in the shrug of his wide shoulders. 'If I were you, I'd reserve judgment until you do.'

'I've met Amanda. I can see it won't be easy to

establish good relations with her, but she isn't happy, and at sixteen she should be.'

'Don't talk like a fool,' he retorted. 'Teenagers are never happy.'

'They may be volatile,' Laura flung back. 'But they shouldn't be in a state of rebellion all the time.'

His eyes ran over her demure brown suit, her smooth blonde head and the long legs discreetly crossed as she sat back in her chair. She saw his brows wing upward and faint amusement touched his face.

'I've no doubt you were a model adolescent, not a touch of rebellion anywhere, but you mustn't base your judgments on yourself.'

Laura flushed and glared at him. 'How well do *you* know her?'

His eyes hardened. 'I'm a busy man.'

'So I've been told,' said Laura with a dry glance.

'Well, I'm telling you now,' he stressed with a narrowed and antagonistic stare. 'I have to pack the work of ten men into every day. I've learnt to delegate wherever I can, but far too many of the daily decisions still fall within my own province. I haven't got time to supervise my daughter's life. When my wife died Amanda was only four. It seemed natural to let my mother take charge of her and she has been doing so ever since.'

'Do you still think it was the best decision?' Laura asked without intonation.

He half closed his eyes on an irritable sigh. 'Miss Crawford, we aren't here so that you can put me through an inquisition. I wanted to see you to discuss the best way of dealing with Amanda now.'

'Until I know her better I can't hazard a guess,' Laura observed levelly.

He pushed back his chair and stood up, towering over her. He was over six feet, she decided, a long lean man with wide shoulders and the tapering hips of someone in the peak of condition. His dark suit was smoothly tailored and cut to emphasise the slim build beneath it. Staring at her fixedly, he pushed his hands into his pockets and rocked on his heels, obviously deep in thought.

After a moment he said: 'I can't make up my mind whether you can handle her or not. It seems to me that you're far too soft. I'd expected you to be more level-headed. You're a nurse, I gathered?'

'Yes,' said Laura with a deepening sensation of hostility towards him. 'I'm a staff nurse and I'm level-headed enough to run a ward full of very sick people, so I imagine I'm capable of looking after one teenage girl, however difficult.'

'One would have thought so,' he said in the tones of someone who very much doubts it.

'One would be quite right,' Laura muttered.

Their eyes clashed. For a second she thought she saw laughter in his, but then he looked away and his face betrayed no sign of amusement whatever.

'When Amanda was a child she had a succession of nurses,' he went on brusquely. 'Then she had a governess until she went to school, but none of them seemed able to deal with her. They came and went all the time.'

'That must have done a lot for her sense of stability,' Laura commented.

'There you go again,' he bit out. 'You jump to too many conclusions and on too little evidence.'

'I'm basing my view on the evidence you're giving me yourself,' she pointed out.

He eyed her as though he was beginning to get really irritated with her. 'This sort of discussion isn't getting us very far. I am not under any obligation to excuse myself to you, Miss Crawford. Amanda's own character is as much at fault as her upbringing, remember.'

'Is it?'

He turned on his heel, making an explosive noise under his breath which did not quite resolve itself into actual speech.

With his back to her he demanded: 'Do you want the job or not?'

'Yes,' said Laura.

'Then for God's sake stop sniping at me,' he said, and turned to face her again, giving her that hard inimical stare.

'I hope you are going to be as obstinate with Amanda as you have been with me,' he remarked.

'I'm obstinate with everyone,' Laura said, smiling at him.

He watched the blue eyes, sunlight picking out the bright gleam of them and turning her smooth hair to a fine gilt frame around her face.

'If I'm to help Amanda, I have to understand her. She has to be sure I'm on her side,' Laura said.

'I was beginning to suspect you were,' he said drily.

'I won't get her to trust me if she thinks that I'm going to be running to you or your mother with news of everything she says or does.'

He sat down and gazed at her unreadably. A light flickered on the console beside his elbow, and Laura glanced aside at it in surprise. She saw his head turn, the dark eyes observe the light and then, ignoring it, glance back at her.

'In other words, you're demanding a free hand with her?'

Laura considered that. 'Within certain terms of reference, yes.'

'And the terms of reference are?'

'That I should keep her out of trouble if I can,' said Laura, smiling at him.

'And if she gets into trouble anyway?'

'Try to get her out of it.'

'Without, as you put it, running to myself or my mother?'

'Exactly.'

'You ask a good deal.'

'I'm asking you to trust me,' she agreed.

'That makes it sound very simple, but it isn't. This is my daughter you are talking about and you want carte blanche with your handling of her. Why should I give it to you?'

Laura looked back at him calmly. 'That's up to you, of course.'

'And if I refuse, you won't take the job?'

She nodded.

He drummed his fingers in that brusque, impatient movement again. 'I got you over here to interview you, but I get the feeling the boot was on the other foot.'

Laura didn't comment on that. The light on the console began to flash again and again he regarded it without attempting to do anything about it.

'Am I allowed to ask precisely what plans you do have for her?'

'I don't have any,' Laura admitted in frank amusement. 'I don't see how I could possibly make any until I know her. That's the first step, isn't it?'

For a long moment he went on staring at her. 'Maybe you'll let me have a memo of what you find out,' he said at last, and put out a hand to flick a switch on the console. 'Yes, what is it, George?'

'New York, sir,' said a soft voice.

'Put them on.' He glanced at Laura. 'I'd appreciate it if you would remember that despite appearances I do care what happens to my daughter,' he said as he reached out his hand for the white phone.

Laura caught the tone of dismissal and rose. He nodded to her and spoke into the phone. 'Joe? Hi.'

Laura heard the door open as she moved towards it. George Ryan stood back to let her pass, giving her his neutral smile. He closed the door on the quick, deep voice and ushered her back down the corridor to the lift.

'Your passport is in order, Miss Crawford?' he enquired as they went down to the ground floor.

'Yes, it is.'

'Have you travelled much?' he asked, watching her.

'I've been abroad several times, but only on brief holidays.'

The lift halted and the door opened. Laura walked to the main entrance with George Ryan at her side. Making sure she left? she wondered. Or merely being polite?

He opened the door and gave her a half bow. 'It was very pleasant to meet you, Miss Crawford. Good afternoon.'

Laura did not bother to take another taxi. She caught a bus after a short wait and made her way home in a stream of homegoing traffic which was building up now to a positive flood.

Beth slumped down on her own bed a couple of hours later, her eyes shut, moaning, 'My feet!'

'Bad day?'

'Hectic. It was one of those days when everything goes wrong. The steriliser nearly blew up and one of the students had hysterics. A kidney transplant came in and there was a mix-up. He nearly got prepped for surgery as gallstones. On top of that I got runs in two pair of stockings, one on the laundry basket and the other on a stool in the canteen.'

Laura began to laugh. 'Compared to that my day was sheer tranquillity,' she admitted.

Beth sat up, eyes flying open. 'I'd forgotten all about that. What happened? What was she like?'

'I'm not sure. Very well preserved, as Henry would say, and I think I liked her, but I'm not certain.'

Beth gave her a look and an exasperated groan. 'What was the hotel like? I've never even been inside, but I've seen it from the outside.'

'Luxury,' Laura mocked. 'She's got a damned great suite high up looking over the park and it's furnished like something in a magazine. You can tell that no ordinary human being lives there. Inside twenty-four hours one normal child could destroy it.'

'Oh,' Beth wailed enviously, 'why didn't I see it?'

'Because you weren't there?' Laura asked, tongue in cheek.

Beth ignored her. 'What was she wearing, Mrs Grey?'

'Something pink, I seem to remember.'

'God give me patience. Something pink!'

'Somehow the jewellery obscured it,' Laura said with a faint dryness.

'What jewellery? Well, go on,' Beth urged. 'Don't tell me you didn't notice that!'

'I noticed it,' Laura admitted. 'Diamonds, mostly, and lots of them. Far too many, to my mind, but it's a question of taste, I suppose.' She paused. 'Not to mention availability. If you have them I suppose you might as well wear them.'

'I would,' Beth said frankly. 'Even in the bath.'

Laura laughed. 'That would take the shine off them pretty fast!'

'Was she haughty?' Beth asked in a faraway tone.

'No,' Laura said in surprise. 'She was friendly and rather nervous, I thought.'

Beth looked disappointed. Laura wondered what images had been floating through her mind.

'And the girl? What was she like? As bad as expected?'

Laura hesitated. 'No,' she said slowly. 'I felt rather sorry for her.'

'Your reactions just aren't normal,' Beth pointed out. 'She's stinking rich and from what Henry says she's spoilt and difficult. Why should you feel sorry for her?' Without waiting for an answer she went on to answer the question herself. 'I know—poor little rich girl. Don't give me that. I don't buy it. She probably loves to make them all run around in circles. That's what gives her her kicks.'

Laura did not bother to argue. Beth had not seen Amanda's face or the sullen droop of her mouth, her flaring bitterness towards her father when he arrived.

'No sign of Daddy, I suppose?' Beth went on to ask wistfully.

'He did turn up,' said Laura, enjoying the double take Beth did and the excited glitter of her eyes.

'You're having me on!'

'No.'

'You met him?'

'I spent an hour with him alone today,' Laura told her in teasing tones.

Beth fell backwards on the bed, arms flung wide. 'And she saves it till last!' She sat up again, her face flushed with excitement. 'What's he like? What did he say? What do you mean, you spent an hour alone with him? Where? Laura, what happened?'

Laura laughed and gave her a tormenting look. 'Make me some coffee and I'll tell you everything.'

'Blackmailer!' Beth rushed off to make the coffee,

though, and was back in a few moments with two mugs.

'Well, spill,' she invited, her eyes as round as saucers.

When Laura had finished, Beth asked: 'Is he as good-looking as his press photos?'

'Passable.'

'Come off it,' Beth said knowingly. 'You got a distinct look in your eye when you were talking about him. He's more than passable, right?'

'Right,' Laura said ruefully. 'And he knows it.'

Beth sat up. 'Did he flirt with you?'

'Don't be crazy—I'm not on his list of eligibles,' Laura retorted. 'He was terse and businesslike.' But that hadn't stopped him running those cynical dark eyes over her once or twice, she remembered. Domenicos Aegethos had inspected her—and decided she didn't interest him, she suspected, which was galling.

'Did you fancy him?'

'I wouldn't have him on a plate with an apple in his mouth,' Laura told her firmly. The chief impact Domenicos had made on her was a feeling of hostility. His impatient manner and driving energy didn't turn her on. If she had allowed him to dictate the course of that interview he would have swept her before him like an invading army. No doubt he was used to issuing orders in that curt voice and having people jump to do as they were told.

'You're in a minority of one, then,' said Beth, stretching with a weary yawn. 'He has girls in every corner of the world, if the press is to be believed.'

'I expect it is,' Laura agreed. 'I can believe it; but as far as I'm concerned he lacks charm. I don't like his attitude to his daughter—or his mother, come to that. I got the feeling they were both scared of him. He's as tough as blazes and hasn't got a shred of ordinary human feeling.'

'But he's given you a free hand with the girl,' Beth pointed out.

'I hope he meant it—but I wouldn't mind betting that at the first hint of trouble he'll come down on me like the wolf on the fold.'

CHAPTER THREE

FROM the windows of the apartment you could stare down into the shaded green walks of the Bois de Boulogne. It was one of the most exclusive areas of Paris, a highly desirable place to live. The apartment was in a modern split-level block with huge picture windows and soaring white walls which gave an impression of space and light. It belonged to the Aegethos company and was used by most of the family when they visited Paris.

At night Laura could hear the distant roar of Paris traffic as cars took the road out of the city which threaded the Bois. She lay listening to it like a child listening to the sound of the sea in a shell, lulled to sleep by it. It was the background music of her life. She was a city-bred girl who had grown up with that dull, ceaseless roar in her ears, and she would have missed it if it hadn't been there.

They had been in Paris for two weeks. The days had already taken on a familiar pattern: each morning Laura had breakfast with Amanda while Mrs Grey ate breakfast in bed. All of them had the same— a light continental meal with orange juice, coffee and croissants. Afterwards Amanda and Laura went out sightseeing and shopping together while Mrs Grey got up in a leisurely fashion and went off to do the rounds of the great fashion houses.

'Not me,' Amanda had announced on their first

day. 'I'm not wearing any of that stuff.' She preferred
to buy her clothes in dark little boutiques in odd
corners of the city. 'I'd rather be seen wearing sackcloth and ashes.'

'I *thought* that was sackcloth,' Laura had
murmured, eyeing the dull brown weave of
Amanda's dress, and there had been a stunned
silence.

Mrs Grey had drawn a nervous breath, but
Amanda, after that astonished pause, had grinned.

'Oh, you think you're so clever, don't you?'

It had been far less difficult for Laura to make
friends with the other girl than she had expected.
Amanda, it had turned out, had a sense of humour.
She hid it beneath her heavy make-up and sullen
expression, but it was there, lurking like a pearl in an
oyster shell, and once Laura had realised it they had
had the beginning of a friendship between them.

Amanda was lonely. She would have died rather
than admit it, but her constant changes of school,
her restless, difficult temperament, had left her
almost entirely without friends. She had never had
anyone to talk to and had bottled up all her resentment, pain and anger inside herself. The pressure of
those unrelieved feelings showed in her small, sallow
face, and it was that pressure which had led to her
outbreaks of defiant behaviour.

Laura had had to work at it, of course. Amanda
wasn't giving her trust to anyone without some proof
that they were genuine. She would talk to Laura for
half an hour or so in a lively, friendly fashion, only to
withdraw, her face going sulky again, as though she

was afraid to let herself like anybody.

It was one of her prickly moments which finally cemented their friendship. Eyeing Laura scathingly she had said one day: 'Your clothes are terrible. They make you look like an off-duty nurse.'

'That's what I am,' Laura had pointed out mildly.

'I don't want to go around with an off-duty nurse,' Amanda had sulked. 'People will think I'm a baby.'

'Who would think that?' Laura had drawled, giving her a sly smile.

Amanda had tried to hide her involuntary grin. 'Why don't you get some real gear?' she had asked.

'What does that mean?' Laura had felt an uneasy qualm at the sudden sparkle of mischief which had appeared in the younger girl's dark eyes.

'Come on . . .'

Dragged to one of Amanda's favourite boutiques, Laura had been kitted out with what Amanda felt to be more suitable clothes; a pile of over-tight jeans, baggy pants and brief cotton tops.

Laura saw that, in order to get anywhere with Amanda, she was going to have to disguise herself, make Amanda feel more at ease with her.

Mrs Grey stared in disbelief next day when the two girls appeared at her bedside as she was eating her croissant and cherry jam.

'How do I look?' Laura had asked, eyes amused.

Mrs Grey ran a slow eye over her camelhair pants, belted at the waist with a wide white belt, her pale cream silk shirt and the short jacket she wore over it.

'Charming,' she had mumbled doubtfully.

'Great, isn't it?' Amanda had insisted. 'We're

going to Versailles today. Want to come, Grandma?'

'No, thank you, dear,' Mrs Grey said ruefully. 'Too tiring.'

Later that afternoon, Laura lay back in a chair under the shade of a wide-branched sycamore tree, groaning: 'I'm dead! I couldn't walk another step. How many rooms has that place got?'

'Too many,' Amanda agreed, staring towards the white walls of the palace. 'I guess he had an army of servants, old Louis the Fourteenth.'

They had spent hours tramping around the gilt-encrusted state rooms, following a long trail of other tourists, but first they had had to queue for an hour merely to get into the palace. It was a hot day. The sun blazed down on their heads and people around them drank Coke out of cans all the time or ate icecream. Behind them loomed an equestrian statue of Louis XIV, waving an irate arm towards the army of tourists and apparently yelling: 'Clear off' without making any impression on them as they streamed past him in their jeans and T-shirts, bound for a quick trip around his palace.

Laura could see the statue from the café where she and Amanda were sitting. 'There's the French Revolution in a nutshell,' she said.

'The whole of modern history,' agreed Amanda. 'He looks like King Canute trying to stop the tide.'

'And it just washes over him.'

'Serves him right,' said Amanda, looking disgusted. 'Selfish old monster. What did he want a pad that size for? You couldn't even walk round it in an afternoon.'

'He probably rode round it on his horse,' someone said from the next table, and Amanda began to laugh, her dark eyes dancing.

Laura shot a look at the strangers. They did not look dangerous, but she was responsible for Amanda's safety. The boy who had spoken shuffled his chair sideways, grinning.

'Been inside?' he asked.

'Can't you tell?' Amanda had kicked off her shoes and was wriggling her toes in an exaggerated fashion. 'I may never walk again. I began to think we'd never get out.'

'I thought it was all rather vulgar,' the boy said.

'All that gold,' Amanda agreed, nodding.

'And the rooms are so big.'

'Enormous. What the servants needed were skateboards. Can't you just see them whizzing from one room to another with bowls of soup?'

They grinned at each other. Laura looked at the boy's companion and found him watching her. He was slim and rather elegantly dressed, although he had removed his pale grey jacket and undone his shirt collar, his olive skin flushed with the heat.

'I hope we're not intruding,' he said, smiling. His English was extremely fluent, but that accent was unmistakable and if she had missed it she would have known by his whole appearance that he was French. There was charming cynicism in his features, lively interest flashing in his dark eyes. He had the poised energy of someone used to life in a great city. Even after two weeks, Laura had realised that Paris was a dynamo throbbing at full power night and day.

There was a constant sense of impatience running through everyone you met in the streets. Parisians lived at top speed, pushing themselves to keep up the pace.

Amanda answered for her while she was wondering how to phrase an answer politely. Laura did not want to get into talk with any strangers. Her job was to make sure Amanda did not meet anyone who hadn't been carefully vetted by her grandmother.

'Not at all. It's nice to talk to someone in your own language. Have you noticed that nobody in Paris speaks a word of English?'

The man laughed. 'They may not admit to it,' he agreed. 'I apologise. That is our famous chauvinism. They understand you perfectly, but they are determined not to let the English get away with it.'

'Away with what?' Amanda asked, puzzled.

'Taking over the world.'

Amanda grimaced. 'I'd hardly say we were trying to do that any more.'

'The English language is like moss—put it down anywhere and it spreads. We keep trying to root it out of our own language, but it just pops up again somewhere else. *Franglais* . . . a horrible hybrid, neither one thing nor the other. *Le bifsteak* . . . *le weekend*. Can you blame us for refusing to pander to you?'

Although he had answered Amanda he was looking at Laura, his face teasing, and she answered before she had time to think.

'What about the French words we've borrowed? It doesn't bother us. English accommodates words very easily. Surely a language should be a living organism, constantly adapting and changing? After all, we make room for other modern improvements in our lives from deep-freezers to television satellites—why not in our languages?'

Amanda nodded approvingly. 'The world's getting smaller all the time.'

'I wouldn't say that was necessarily a good thing,' the older man said seriously. 'I think the whole trouble with the world today is loss of identity. People are no longer sure who they are or where they belong. Language isn't really a means of communication—it is a way of establishing identity. After all, what do we mean when we say of someone that they speak our language? We mean we feel at home with them.'

Amanda fluttered her eyelashes at the boy. 'Don't you feel at home with us?' she asked him, and he grinned at her.

'Are you staying in Paris?'

'Yes, do you live here?'

He nodded. 'How long are you staying?'

She shrugged. 'We haven't made up our minds. Another week or two, I expect.'

'Then you go home? Where do you live?'

'London, but we're going on to Italy when we leave Paris.'

'A long holiday,' the man commented, staring at Laura. 'You are sisters?' His voice indicated surprise, and Amanda began to laugh.

'Friends,' she said hurriedly, before Laura could say a word, her dark eyes daring her to give any other explanation. Amanda was very touchy on the subject of Laura's role in her life. She didn't want anyone knowing that her family thought she should have an adult trailing around with her wherever she went. 'I'm Amanda, this is Laura,' she added, pausing expectantly.

'Pierre,' the boy said at once. 'And this is my Uncle Marcel. I'm staying with him while my parents are in Algiers on holiday.'

'Which is why we're here,' Marcel said drily. 'I was dragged out to see Versailles because Pierre had nothing else to do. The fact that I was very busy was of no importance.'

Pierre made a face at Amanda. 'All he thinks about is work.'

'I know the type,' she said. 'My father . . .'

'Once they're thirty they think of nothing but making money,' Pierre agreed.

'And what do you think about?' asked Marcel. 'Spending it?'

'Ho-ho,' Amanda jeered. 'That's what is known as an adult sense of humour.'

'I think about sex,' Pierre said, looking at her slyly.

She laughed, eyes dancing.

'He's honest, anyway,' Marcel murmured to Laura, who was feeling rather alarmed. She looked at her watch and gave a loud exclamation.

'Good heavens, look at the time!'

Amanda got that obstinate look again. 'So what? We're in no hurry to get back.'

'How did you get here? We came by car. Can we give you a lift back?' Pierre looked hopefully at Amanda. He was a very thin boy with short, curly black hair, enormous dark eyes and a tanned skin. His eyes gave him a permanently pleading expression, even when he smiled, and it was hard not to like him. He had the appeal of a lost dog.

'We came by taxi and we'd love a lift back,' Amanda said at once.

'That's very kind, but no, thank you,' said Laura, trying to override her without sounding unfriendly. She smiled at Marcel. 'We can easily get a taxi back.'

His eyes narrowed understandingly and she saw him shrug. Pierre, though, did not accept her answer.

'No, no, why bother to take taxis when you can have a more comfortable ride with us? They charge the earth from here.' He got up. 'The car's in the car park over there.'

Amanda was on her feet too. The waiter came rushing over to give Laura the bill. Looking after Amanda impatiently, she took it, but it was removed from her grasp. Marcel paid both bills, giving her a wry smile.

'You'll be quite safe, I promise you. I'm not a dangerous driver and the car *is* very comfortable.'

Flushing, she half apologised. 'I'm sure it is. It's very kind of you.'

He read the hesitation in her tone. 'You don't need to worry, you know. We're a very respectable pair and we aren't planning to kidnap you both and lock you up in a brothel.'

'I didn't think you were,' she said, beginning to laugh.

'No?' He sounded dubious and she shook her head firmly.

'It never crossed my mind. It's just that I'm responsible for Amanda and . . .' She stopped, because how could you say politely that you felt you had to be careful about someone?

'And you would like some references?' Marcel finished for her calmly, his expression un-insulted. 'I am a businessman. I own several shops and a small hotel in Paris. Pierre's father is my partner in the hotel. We come highly recommended, I assure you.' His amusement wrinkled his nose and made lines stretch on either side of his eyes and mouth. Laura's caution clearly gave him cause for laughter and she had to smile back.

No doubt it did seem funny to him, but she couldn't tell him frankly why she had to be so careful about Amanda. It would be best if he did not know that Amanda's father was so wealthy.

With her tight jeans and casual, friendly manner Amanda didn't give the impression of being the spoilt daughter of a millionaire, which was all to the good.

They reached the car and found the two young people arguing hotly about pop music. They argued about it all the way to Paris along the autoroute. Marcel made little effort to compete with the noisy duet in the back. Now and then he smiled at Laura and made some polite remark, but obviously he had taken her reluctance to come back with them personally and he left her to her thoughts most of the way.

When he drew up outside the apartment block

Pierre looked up at it and exclaimed: 'Wow! You're staying here?'

Amanda looked more alive than she usually did, her face glowing with colour. She nodded, diving out of the car. 'Thanks for the lift,' she said as Laura got out too. ' 'Bye.'

Laura was surprised by the casual way she wandered off. She looked after her and then gave Marcel a polite smile. 'Thank you. Nice to have met you.'

His face was wry. 'And you,' he said, starting the engine again. The car drew away and Laura followed Amanda into the apartment block. The lift arrived just as Laura did and they walked into it.

She watched Amanda press the button. 'Pierre was a pleasant boy,' she said carefully.

Amanda didn't rise to it. She shrugged. 'I wonder if there'll be langoustine on the menu again tonight. I enjoyed that last night.'

Laura was under no illusions. Her fishing had been deliberately evaded. It wasn't part of her brief to investigate Amanda's inner feelings, so she left it. She would have expected her to take rather longer over her goodbyes, but maybe Pierre had offended her during that long wrangle over pop music. You could never tell with Amanda what was going on inside her head. She was a touchy girl. Laura decided to drop the subject.

Mrs Grey was feeling rather more lively this evening. When they joined her she asked about their day in a perfunctory manner before excitedly telling them that she had had a telephone call from her husband who would be joining them in Italy. Laura had met Barney Grey briefly. He looked rather like one of his own sausages, pink and smooth and slightly plastic, but she had got the feeling that he had a kind heart. He seemed to regard Amanda as if she were an un-exploded firework, but at the same time he had an air of baffled concern towards her. Laura had the idea that he was an amiable man with very little imagination who would have liked to make friends with Amanda but didn't have a clue where to start. As for Amanda's views about him, it was true that she had yawned when he tried to tell her how de-lightful Paris could be in summer and had sighed heavily when he warned her not to wander off alone, but somehow there hadn't been any special hostility in her face. Barney Grey wasn't positive enough to arouse anything more in Amanda than her usual worldweary adolescent scorn for adults.

'And I'm going to dinner with friends tonight,' Mrs Grey said. 'So you two will have to dine alone.'

'We'll survive,' Amanda told her patronisingly. 'You run along and have a great time, Grand-mother.'

'Isn't she thoughtful?' Laura asked Mrs Grey drily.

'Oh, you!' Amanda said, grinning.

'Are you sure you don't mind?' Mrs Grey asked, looking from one to the other smilingly.

'Just be careful and don't come back too late,' said Amanda. 'And don't drink too much or pick up any strange men.'

Mrs Grey moved away, smiling. Amanda was in a

very good mood this evening, Laura thought, watching her. She saw her put a hand to her forehead, frowning.

'Headache?' Laura asked in surprise.

'A bit of one—it must be the sun.'

'It was hot today,' Laura agreed.

'I think I'll have an early night,' Amanda said. 'But first I want to see if there is langoustine on the menu tonight.'

'If you're not feeling too well it would be a mistake to eat shellfish before going to bed,' Laura pointed out.

'Stop coming on the heavy nurse with me,' Amanda retorted. 'Shellfish doesn't bother me. And I'm starving.'

The housekeeper apologised sadly. No langoustine. She had a terrine of lobster, she suggested; so Amanda kindly settled for that with a sigh. After they had kissed Mrs Grey goodnight and seen her off to her dinner party they had dinner alone and then Amanda collected up a huge pile of magazines and went off to bed. Laura gave her half an hour and then went into the bedroom to check that she wasn't suffering anything worse than mild headache. The light was out and Amanda was just a little hump in the bed. Laura listened to her regular breathing before tiptoeing out again and quietly closing the door.

She changed into a loose kaftan and washed her hair, blow-drying it while she watched an old silent movie on the TV. It was a horror film which relied for its effects on huge, looming shadows and an expression of dazed terror on the heroine's face every time she looked round. Laura had the giggles by the time it had ended. She switched off the set and was about to go to bed when the lounge door opened and she looked round in shock, jumping visibly.

'I'm sorry, did I startle you?' She had had the lights low while she watched the film and for a second the dark shadow in the doorway had made her heart stop. It strolled forward and she recognised Domenicos Aegethos, which should have slowed her pulse rate, but which oddly had the effect of accelerating it. Laura didn't have time to speculate on this strange phenomenon. She hurriedly rearranged her face into a polite expression.

'Good evening, Mr Aegethos. I didn't realise you were expected.' She knew he hadn't been. His mother would have mentioned it. Did he make a habit of dropping in unannounced? The day she had first met him she had got the feeling that his Jack-in-the-box arrival was typical and deliberate. He liked taking his mother by surprise.

'I wasn't,' he said drily. 'Where is my mother?'

'Mrs Grey is out to dinner with friends,' Laura told him, adding carefully, 'Amanda is in bed.' A pity I didn't go to bed too, she thought. I could have avoided seeing him until the morning and I might have felt more capable of dealing with him then.

'At this hour?' His brows rose sharply. 'Is she ill? Or just sulking?'

'Neither. She had a headache. We went to Versailles today. It was very hot and we walked quite a way. Amanda was feeling frayed at the edges.'

His eyes took on a derisive amusement. 'But not you? You took it in your stride, did you? You look as cool as a cucumber.'

'I enjoyed it,' said Laura, the back of her neck prickling as he swept that slow, appraising gaze over her black kaftan as though he could see right through it. Has he got X-ray eyes? she wondered. His glance came back to her face and took in the expression it wore. His mouth twisted.

'Very fetching,' he said, and he was mocking her, the sexual nature of his inspection quite deliberate. Laura resented that look. Her face froze.

'The housekeeper has gone to bed too,' she said coolly. 'Have you eaten? Can I get you anything?'

'I've eaten,' he said, looking round the spacious modern room. 'I'd like a drink, though.' He walked towards the long cabinet which held drinks. 'Can I get you something? What would you like?'

'Nothing, thank you. I was just on my way to bed.' She hovered, watching him open the cabinet. Over his shoulder he said calmly: 'Nonsense, have a nightcap.'

'No, thank you.' She stared at his wide shoulders, the smooth fit of his jacket drawing the eye down his long back. Even when he was standing still he gave the impression of restless energy, but it was a dynamism harnessed by the mind inside that black head. Domenicos Aegethos had all that energy under control. She did not get the feeling that he was a man who gave way to impulse. He knew very well what he was doing and why and he did it deliberately. Laura found that slightly alarming.

When he turned he had two glasses in his hands. He held one out to her, his dark eyes sardonic.

'I don't want a drink, thank you,' she said impatiently.

'It will help you sleep.'

'I don't need that sort of help.'

'You're lucky.' He put one glass down and tilted the other to his mouth, watching her as he swallowed some of the brandy.

'Goodnight, Mr Aegethos,' she said, edging towards the door.

'Not going, surely?' he drawled. 'I was expecting that memo on Amanda.'

'Tonight?' she asked in surprise.

'No time like the present.' He beckoned with a long index finger, a faint mockery in his eyes, and Laura reluctantly walked back towards him and sat down on the sofa. He stood over her, his glass in his hand, studying her as if she were a strange specimen under a microscope.

'So, how are you getting on with her?'

'I think we're making progress. It took some time for her to get used to me. She wasn't exactly thrilled to have me in tow all day, but we seem to have got over her initial resentment. I have no worries.'

'Good,' he said, sitting down next to her. 'How much time does my mother spend with her?'

Laura's eyes opened in surprise. 'Most evenings.'

'But not the days?'

'We've been sightseeing quite a bit and Mrs Grey gets tired rather quickly.'

His mouth twisted. 'Doesn't she?'

There was something odd about the way he said that. Laura frowned. 'She is seventy.' Why was she excusing his mother to him, for heaven's sake? He knew his mother was seventy. Surely he didn't expect a woman of her age to go trotting around Paris tourist spots like a teenager?

He took off the jacket of his well cut dark suit and slung it casually across the arm of the sofa. She watched him stretch, his long legs draped across the floor, his arms reaching above his black head.

'I've had a long day,' he said, catching her eye. 'I'm dead tired.'

'Travelling is tiring,' Laura agreed, getting up again.

His hand shot out to catch her wrist. 'Not so fast,' he said. 'Do you mind? I need to unwind. Talk to me.'

Nothing like giving orders, Laura thought rebelliously, looking at his lean fingers as they tightened on her.

'I thought you were tired.'

'I am—too tired to go to bed yet. Haven't you ever been that tired?'

'Frequently,' she said drily.

'And what do *you* do?'

'Take a warm bath and go to bed,' she said, smiling.

'Imaginative,' he drawled, sudden amusement in his eyes. 'Why don't we do just that?'

For a second she was too taken aback to react, then a slight flush ran into her face as she took in the implication.

'Not tonight, thank you,' she said calmly.

His laughter was genuine. 'Not a hair out of place,' he said.

Laura stared.

'I wondered what reaction I'd get,' he informed her wickedly.

'What were you expecting?'

'I wasn't sure. A prim shudder, perhaps? A stifled scream? Or even a slapped face.' He released her wrist and patted the sofa. 'Sit down—I don't bite. Tell me what you thought of Versailles.'

'It's unbelievable,' she said simply.

He finished his drink. 'Well? Go on. That's interesting, but it hardly does justice to the subject.'

'What could? Versailles is beautiful, but quite unreal—a sort of French Disneyland. I kept expecting Mickey Mouse to come trotting out of a door, or to find Louis the Fourteenth selling popcorn in the courtyard.'

'Give it time,' he grinned. 'They'll think of that.'

He undid his tie and dropped it beside his jacket, then undid his waistcoat. 'Tell me,' he asked interestedly, 'when you stop work what do you really do?'

'I told you, have a bath and go to bed.'

'And then you sleep like a log, I suppose?'

She nodded.

'Incredible! I envy you. I sleep very badly—I'm an insomniac. How do you manage it?'

'Mine is a tiring job.'

'So,' he said wryly, 'is mine, but I still can't get to sleep.' He started undoing his shirt and she watched with alarm. How much more undressing did he plan to do?

'And do you always sleep alone?' he enquired with what seemed no more than mild curiosity.

'That's a very personal question.'

'Isn't it?' He smiled at her sideways, his eyes amused. 'But how about an answer? Purely academic, I assure you. I'm just curious. What sort of sex life do nurses get?'

'The same sort as everybody else, except that we have less time for it.'

He slid a smile towards her, the dark eyes roaming from her blonde head to her feet and lingering here and there on the way down, the appraisal lazily inviting. 'I'm quite sure you get plenty of offers,' he said. 'You're a very attractive girl.'

'Thank you,' she said, registering his smile thoughtfully. She didn't need to have him draw any diagrams, and she wasn't surprised when he shifted closer, his arm moving along the back of the sofa. He had undone the top three buttons of his shirt and his collar lay open, giving her a clear view of his smooth brown throat and the short curly black hair on his chest.

'And you have plenty of time, now,' he added, his eyes teasing her.

'Time but no inclination,' she returned with calm gravity. She supposed it was rather flattering to have him make a light pass, but somehow she wasn't flattered. He was tired and wanted to be amused, and she was a woman and might be available. It was a simple enough equation. He wasn't using any pressure. The proposition just hovered in the air between them. No doubt this was what they called sophistication. Laura didn't think too much of it.

He raised a casual hand and ran cool fingertips down the side of her cheek, tracing the structure of the fine bones. 'You might enjoy it,' he said, his fingers reaching her mouth and one of them trailing softly along the curve of it.

For some reason she found that oddly disturbing. There was a distinct sense of control about him, an awareness of what he was doing which suggested that he knew what effect he could have on a woman if he played this slow, sensual game. The smiling dark eyes, the warm husky voice, the caressing touch of that hand, added up to a formidable weaponry, but although Laura's lips tingled at the delicate brush of his fingertip she refused to let such deliberate sexual needling affect her.

'Bloodless sex doesn't turn me on,' she told him, her blue eyes cool.

His brows went up. 'Bloodless?'

'How else would you describe it? I know you need to unwind, but I'm not flattered to be regarded as some sort of tranquilliser.'

He laughed. 'I must be slipping if I gave the impression that that was how I saw you,' he said with amusement, taking light hold of her chin and bending towards her with very obvious intentions.

She pulled back, shaking her head, a hand on his chest to hold him at arm's length.

'No, thank you, Mr Aegethos. I'm just not into casual sex. It wouldn't mean anything to either of us, would it? So why bother?'

He leaned back again, shrugging, his mouth rueful. 'Okay,' he said, accepting it without a show of temper, which she found quite likeable. 'Shall we change the subject? What made you become a nurse?'

She laughed at the abrupt change of course, but began to answer, and surprised herself by telling him about the crash in which her parents had died. He surprised her even more by listening intently. She found him a persuasive listener. The dark eyes absorbed her as she talked, their steady gaze almost hypnotic, and she found herself telling him things she couldn't remember ever telling anyone before. Laura was not someone who confided easily in people. Somehow, without asking a single question, Domenicos Aegethos drew words out of her, and when she paused at last she was astonished by how much she had told him.

'You have a very soothing voice,' he said.

Laura began to laugh. 'Well, I'm glad I amused you.' She got up. 'I must go to bed. Goodnight, Mr Aegethos.'

'You might as well call me Nicos,' he said. 'Goodnight, Laura.' The curt impatience which had annoyed her the first time they met was totally missing in him tonight. She walked to the door, thinking that she rather liked him, after all. A glance back at him showed him at ease on the sofa, his black head flung back, his legs stretched out full length. He looked as if he was half asleep already.

In her own room she undressed and got ready for

bed. She put out the light and settled with a sigh, yawning.

Suddenly the door crashed open. The light blazed. Laura sat up, as tense as a coiled spring, looking across the room at him in shock.

It was hard to believe that those dark eyes had ever smiled the way they had earlier. He looked savage, his face hard and angular, his eyes spitting fury at her.

'So there are no problems? You're quite happy with the way Amanda's been behaving? You did say you slept like a log, I believe?' He gave her no chance to ask him what was wrong, sweeping on in an angry voice, 'My God, you stupid bitch, the girl's been running rings round you! I told you to watch her like a hawk. She can't be trusted. I warned you, but you knew better, of course. You swallowed everything she said, hook, line and sinker. Headache?' He laughed. 'It may interest you to know that Amanda is not in her bed with a headache. She isn't in the apartment at all. God knows where she is—but she's certainly made a fool of you!'

CHAPTER FOUR

LAURA digested what he had said, frowning anxiously. 'She isn't in her room?'

'Don't you understand English?' he roared, and why she had ever thought he was a controlled man she did not know. That sophisticated, civilised exterior had cracked and something far more elemental was showing through. He might treat other women lightly, but where the women of his family were concerned he had a violent reaction.

'If you'll wait for me in the lounge I'll join you,' Laura said. No way was she getting out of that bed with him watching her. She was wearing bedtime gear which Amanda had picked out for her—a baseball shirt that only reached the top of her thighs—and she was not modelling that for him in his present mood.

He looked at her scathingly, his black brows meeting. 'If there's one thing I can't stand it is coy women,' he told her through tight lips, his eyes skating over the part of the baseball shirt he could see, but all the same he turned on his heel and strode out, exuding masculine impatience.

Laura winced as the door crashed shut. She dived out of bed and hurriedly got into a floor-length cotton housecoat which zipped up the front.

When she joined Domenicos he had drawn back the curtains at the great windows and was standing there, staring out over Paris, a glass of whisky in his hand and a look of brooding savagery on his face. Laura waited, watching him, and in a moment he turned to glower at her.

'Do you have any idea where she is?' Before she could open her mouth to answer he snapped: 'The truth, mind. Where is she?'

'I've no idea.' There goes my job, Laura thought. He had his doubts before, but now he'll have me on a plane back to London before I can whistle.

'She wouldn't have gone out on her own. She must be with somebody, and we can be pretty sure that that somebody is male.' His mouth tightened, a dark blood under his skin. 'Who has she been seeing?'

'Nobody,' said Laura, then stopped, her lips parted as she thought of the boy they had met at Versailles. Surely not?

Domenicos had seen her look of surprise and his eyes narrowed. 'You've thought of something? Someone?'

'We did meet a boy at Versailles . . .'

'Oh, you did!' He interrupted, his voice unpleasant. 'What boy? I thought I made it clear that you were to stop Amanda meeting anybody unless you were there too?'

'I was there too, and I certainly didn't encourage it.'

He ignored that. 'What's his name?'

'Pierre,' Laura said, knowing the next question and knowing he was not going to like her answer.

'Pierre what?'

'I don't know,' she muttered.

'You don't know!' He gave her a fulminating look, then walked away and poured himself another whisky. 'How did she get out without you noticing?'

'I've no idea,' Laura admitted. 'Maybe while I was washing my hair.' She was stung by the biting look he gave her and said angrily: 'I can't watch her twenty-four hours a day. What do you want me to do? Sleep across her door?'

'What sort of boy was this?' he asked, ignoring her rhetorical question.

'Rather a nice one.' Their eyes met and she said crossly: 'Well, I liked him. He was pleasant and friendly.'

'I'm sure he was,' he said drily. 'I meet a lot of pleasant and friendly people myself. Money has that effect on people.'

'Oh, don't be ridiculous,' Laura snapped, getting annoyed. 'He didn't know Amanda had money. She wasn't carrying a placard saying: Come and get me, I'm loaded.'

Domenicos did not look either amused or convinced. 'Perhaps now you see why I don't trust her. She picks up a perfect stranger and vanishes with him to God knows where, doing God knows what.' His colour darkened further. 'Except that we can have a pretty shrewd idea what they're doing, if not where, can't we?'

Laura stared at him, her blue eyes wide and cold. 'I think you're jumping to conclusions.'

'Oh, you do?' he sneered, his eyes hostile.

She bristled. 'Yes, I do. Amanda is only just sixteen, and although she may be rebellious I don't see her as some sort of teenage tramp.'

'What do you think she was doing at that all-night party? Playing checkers?'

'Dancing, probably,' snapped Laura, getting angrier. 'Why don't you stop seeing things from your own angle and try seeing them from hers? How much time have you spent with her over the past few years? I'd say I know her better than you do, and you've got entirely the wrong idea of her. If she was a little tramp it would probably be because of your example . . .' She broke off, drawing a shaken breath at what she had said, and his dark eyes glittered with fury.

'*What?*' The word shot out of him at white-hot speed.

'Your own attitude to sex is hardly much to write home about,' Laura added, deciding she had already gone too far to draw back.

'I'm not sixteen,' he grated. 'And who the hell do you think you are, talking to me like that?'

'Children always take their attitudes from the adults around them,' she informed him. 'If Amanda thinks casual sex is fine, that would be your fault. That's what you think, isn't it?'

He seemed to be speechless, staring at her with narrowed eyes.

'Not that I believe she does think that,' Laura went on more calmly. 'You haven't met Pierre—I have. I don't see him seducing her. They're probably sitting out at some street café listening to pop music and talking. At that age it can be exciting just to talk, or wouldn't you remember that?'

He looked at her blankly. No, she thought, he didn't remember that. Maybe he had never known the feeling of breathless excitement that came in your teens when you talked endlessly to friends, discovering yourself as an adult for the first time while you discovered that other people were undergoing the same process. She looked at his hard, dark face: the narrowed eyes, the angular features with that certainty and assertion built into the bone structure, and wondered if he had ever been a troubled adolescent in search of himself. Or had he been an adult in his pram?

'You honestly expect me to believe the girl is just talking to this boy?'

'What's so unbelievable about that? You may see sex as the only point of contact between a man and a woman, but maybe you have no sense of curiosity.'

'Curiosity?' he repeated, staring at her, his mouth twisting.

'Sexual curiosity doesn't have to be physical.'

'But it usually is,' he said drily. 'My God, you have a pure mind!'

'Not pure,' Laura corrected. 'Practical. You're condemning Amanda unheard. Can't you wait until she gets back and let her tell you where she's been and what she's been doing?'

'And I'm supposed to swallow whatever cock-and-bull story she comes up with, I suppose?'

'You'll have to make up your own mind about that after you've heard her out,' Laura shrugged.

His attitude seemed odd to her, all the same. 'You're being over-protective,' she added. 'Most girls of her age go out with boys. What do you expect? You can't keep her locked in a chastity belt until she's legally of age.'

'It's an idea, though,' he said, and now there was a slight trace of humour in his voice and the harshness had softened slightly in his face. He moved restlessly, his hands in his pockets, his head bent. Laura watched him walk towards the window and away again, the pacing energy of his body that of a caged animal. He stopped and swung towards her.

'I'm not in the habit of talking to people about my private life,' he said rapidly. 'But, you see . . .'

A sound interrupted him, and he broke off, looking swiftly towards the door, his body tense. Mrs Grey appeared in the doorway, looking flushed and smiling, a pure white mink wrap folded round her and a silver evening bag gleaming in her hands.

'Nicos,' she said, her smile vanishing and a look of alarm coming into her face.

He had that cold look in his face again. He looked at the tiny jade clock on the table beside him. 'Late, aren't you?' he demanded, taking Laura's breath away.

There was no doubt about it. His attitude was quite extraordinary. From the bristling hostility of his tone you might have imagined he was demanding an explanation from his daughter, not his mother. Surely he didn't imagine that Mrs Grey had been living it up too?

'Is it? Oh, dear. I hadn't noticed the time. When did you get here, Nicos? If I'd known you were coming I wouldn't have gone out.'

'I'm sure you wouldn't,' he snarled.

Mrs Grey took off her wrap and Laura noticed with concern that her hands were trembling.

'Where have you been until this hour?' he asked, watching his mother as she put down her wrap and evening bag and nervously fidgeted with her hair.

Why doesn't she tell him to drop dead? Laura thought. Why does she put up with being spoken to like that? Even more interesting—why does he talk to her like that? She's seventy years old, but he talks to her as if she were seventeen. Why?

'I had dinner with friends,' Mrs Grey faltered.

'Friends? Or a friend?'

Nasty, Laura thought. He was making her skin prickle. What was he doing to his mother?

Mrs Grey looked at him, her sad dark eyes shining as if with unshed tears. 'I think I'll go to bed,' she said with dignity, turning away.

'Amanda has apparently done a bunk again,' Domenicos shot at her abruptly, and she stopped, gasping, to look at Laura.

'What's happened?'

'We don't know yet,' Laura said gently. 'I suspect she's gone out to meet a boy we met at Versailles, but I'm sure she's fine. He was a very nice boy and she'll be perfectly safe with him.'

Domenicos laughed sardonically. 'You live in a dream world!'

'I wouldn't worry,' Laura told Mrs Grey, ignoring him.

'But I don't understand—why did you let her go out?'

Laura explained the whole circumstances and Mrs Grey listened with an agitated face, her hand at her throat clutching her inevitable diamonds, their white flash making the ghastly pallor of her skin even more painful.

'But you mustn't worry,' Laura ended, and Domenicos gave her that scathing smile again.

'No, you mustn't worry, Mama. We wouldn't want you to do that.'

Mrs Grey looked pleadingly at Laura. 'Have you rung the police?'

'It isn't that late,' Laura pointed out. 'She'll be back.'

'She's in a strange city and she's only sixteen,' snapped Domenicos. 'For all we know she's already floating in the Seine!'

'Oh!' groaned Mrs Grey, sagging.

Laura put an arm round her, giving Domenicos an irritated look. 'Don't be so melodramatic.'

'It seems to me that you're taking this whole thing very lightly,' he muttered.

'Somebody has to—you're making far too much of a performance out of it. It's worrying that Amanda should have gone off without telling us where or with whom, but you're going to the other extreme and imagining the worst before you know just what has happened.'

'I've good reason to know what sort of blood runs in her veins,' he said icily, with his eyes on his mother.

Mrs Grey trembled. Laura felt the betraying movement as she supported her and her frown deepened. What was all this about? There was a good deal that was not being said but which both Mrs Grey and her son tacitly understood.

They all heard the closing of the apartment front door. Domenicos whirled out of the room like a flash of lightning, and they heard the explosive roar of his voice. He was talking in Greek, the words deep and harsh and rending.

'Don't let him,' Mrs Grey whispered to her. She gave Laura a little push, her sad eyes begging. 'He shouldn't say such things to her!'

Laura moved uncertainly and Mrs Grey sank down on the sofa. Laura went into the hall and saw Amanda in an off-the-shoulder peasant blouse and jeans facing her father defiantly, her lower lip stuck out in a sullen pout. She wasn't saying a word. He was more than making up for that, and whatever he was saying was making Amanda very angry.

'I hate you!' she suddenly broke out, and ran towards her room.

Her father strode after her. The door slammed and was locked. He halted at it, then turned on his heel and vanished into another room, slamming that door.

Laura slowly went back to Mrs Grey, who was staring at nothing and shivering. Laura sat down beside her and rubbed her hands. They were ice cold and convulsively trembling.

'It's all my fault,' Mrs Grey said wearily.

'Of course it isn't. You mustn't think that. How could it be?' Laura was worried about her. She was far too pale and very cold. Shock could be dangerous at her age.

'Oh, it is, my dear—you just don't know.' Passing a trembling hand over her face Mrs Grey sighed. 'You see, I never loved his father. I didn't even like him. It was an arranged marriage; my family talked me into it. I should have refused, but I suppose I was too weak. He was so very rich and everyone was so excited about it. I gave in, but it didn't work. He wasn't a lovable man, he frightened me.' She looked at Laura soberly. 'Then I got pregnant and when I had some tests the doctors discovered that my blood group was incompatible with my husband's.'

Laura frowned. 'Oh, dear, that was bad luck.'

Mrs Grey's mouth writhed in a bitter smile. 'It seemed symbolic at the time. The baby miscarried, and they said it would always happen. My husband wouldn't believe it. He made me try again and it happened again. My dear, I was so miserably unhappy. It went on for years. He accepted that I couldn't have any more babies, but that meant that he just ignored me.' She looked across the room, her eyes dull. 'They were terrible years.'

Laura thought of the portrait in Domenicos's office, the hard, cold face and chilling eyes. Was there more than a mere facial resemblance between father and son?

Watching Mrs Grey as she stared vacantly at nothing, she prompted: 'But you had Domenicos eventually.'

Mrs Grey started and looked at her in silence, her eyes filled with a depth of unhappiness which made Laura ache with compassion. 'Oh, yes, I had

Domenicos eventually. I didn't even want him at the time. I think a baby knows when a mother feels like that. I was in a state of deep depression when he was born and I couldn't bear to see the baby for months.'

No wonder she carried the fine lines of experience in her face, thought Laura. Poor woman!

'And then it all changed. I met someone.' Mrs Grey sighed. 'Actually I'd known him for years, but it was strange—we suddenly seemed to see each other, and after that it all happened so fast. He was my husband's best friend, he worked for him. I knew my husband would go crazy with rage. I didn't want to lose Domenicos—I'd forgotten by then that I hadn't wanted him. I loved him dearly, he was only eight at the time, and I knew how my husband would react. He would take Domenicos away from me and I'd never see him. It was an unbearable situation.'

'It must have been,' Laura said, frowning. It must have been agonising. What a decision to have to make!

'It all blew up in our faces one night. Stavros and I had to see each other alone now and then, and my husband found out. There was a terrible scene. He hit me and Stavros hit him, and then Stavros and I left together. A week later my husband had a heart attack. He made a will leaving Nicos to the care of his uncle, my husband's brother. The whole Aegethos family detested me. My husband died and they wouldn't let me see Nicos. I married Stavros, but I didn't stop trying to see my son. I knew they must be poisoning his mind against me, but I was helpless. I couldn't get to him.' She looked at Laura, her eyes full of unshed tears. 'I can't tell you how badly I felt about that.'

'Were you happy with your second husband?' Laura asked, her face sympathetic.

Mrs Grey gave a faint smile. 'Very. If it hadn't been for Nicos my life would have been heaven. But Stavros was much older than I was—he died ten years later and I was alone again. Nicos was of age by then, but when I wrote to him he ignored my letters. I think he would never have seen me again if he hadn't married Lina. You see, Lina was my god-daughter. Her mother was a cousin of mine. And it was Lina who talked Nicos into meeting me again.'

'I see,' Laura said slowly, oddly curious about Domenicos's dead wife. 'What was she like?'

'Pretty,' said Mrs Grey, smiling. 'Very pretty; a lively, highly strung girl with big brown eyes. Nicos was very much in love with her and she was with him, but he was always so busy, just like his father, obsessed with work. He left her alone too much.'

Laura's skin went cold. She had a horrible feeling she knew what was coming next.

'It didn't mean anything, I'm certain it didn't, Lina did love Nicos, but she was bored and left to her own devices,' said Mrs Grey, half to herself.

'She got involved with somebody else?'

Mrs Grey sighed. 'I'm not quite sure what happened. Nicos told me very little. There was a lot of talk at the time. Lina was always going around with another man. She went to parties with him and had private little dinners with him. I heard the gossip and I was very worried, but when I tackled her she just laughed and looked excited. I had the feeling she was trying to make Nicos jealous, trying to get his attention.'

'And she got it?' Laura asked drily. Poor girl, I'm sure she did, she thought. How foolish of her. She couldn't have done anything more stupid.

Mrs Grey grimaced. 'Nicos hit the roof, I think. He was bitterly angry.'

I can imagine, Laura thought, very well able to picture the savage expression in those dark eyes.

'Lina left him and took Amanda with her. She was killed six months later. Nicos arrived one night with Amanda and told me to look after her. He didn't want her with him. He couldn't spare the time to run a nursery, he said.'

'Charming,' Laura muttered, frowning.

'He was beside himself. He didn't want to see her, I think. Nicos is a hard man, like his father. Amanda reminded him and he didn't want to remember.'

'He couldn't blame Amanda for what happened,' Laura said with impatience.

'I don't suppose he did. But she was her mother's daughter.' Mrs Grey looked miserably at her. 'Nicos had a very low opinion of women by then.'

'Not surprisingly, I suppose,' said Laura.

'No,' agreed Mrs Grey, sighing. 'He was so young when I left his father, and then when his marriage broke up like that it hammered home the idea that you couldn't trust women.'

'Have you ever discussed it with him? Told him what you've told me?'

'I've tried, but he always refuses to listen, says he

doesn't want to know. Nicos is very daunting in that sort of mood. His father scared me, but Nicos is quite frightening too, in his way.' Mrs Grey looked up as one of the clocks chimed the hour. 'Oh, dear, it's three o'clock! I've kept you out of bed all this time, listening to me—I do apologise.'

'Don't,' said Laura, smiling. 'I hope it helped to talk.'

'It did, my dear,' Mrs Grey said, struggling to her feet. 'Thank you for listening so sympathetically. I'm sorry to bore you with all my problems.'

'It wasn't boring,' Laura assured her as they moved slowly out of the room. 'Goodnight,' she added as Mrs Grey went into her own bedroom, and the other woman whispered back: 'Goodnight, Laura, thank you for being so patient.'

Back in her own room later Laura took off her housecoat and sat up cross-legged on the bed, brooding, her chin propped in her hands. What a mess! If she had had any idea of this background she would never have considered getting involved with them all. She had put down Amanda's rebellion as a typical teenage phase, complicated by her father's indifference. Now she saw it very differently. In a way, Domenicos wasn't far off the mark when he talked about the blood in his daughter's veins, although Laura would have put it rather differently.

What chance of a normal happy life did Amanda have with this tangled emotional background behind her?

You could never cut yourself off from your roots, even if you weren't aware of them consciously.

How much did Amanda know of all this? How much did she guess? And what effect had it had on her?

Switching off the light, she settled to sleep. She was physically exhausted, but her mind was too pre-occupied with all that had happened. She kept slipping towards sleep and jerking awake again. When she did finally sleep it was with a depth that made her wake late, her body stiff and cramped and her skin hot.

She looked at the sunlight dancing on the ceiling. Her head ached and she felt dull. Lately she had been feeling much better, but this morning she was very aware of that creeping weakness which had been the legacy of her bout of pneumonia. She did not feel like getting up.

It was after ten before she left her room. She found Domenicos alone, eating a croissant and drinking black coffee, a newspaper in his hand.

He looked up and gave her a curt nod.

'Good morning,' said Laura, sitting down. She felt the coffee pot and poured herself a cup. Where were Mrs Grey and Amanda? Still in bed? She didn't dare to ask. Let sleeping dogs lie, she thought, taking a croissant.

The silence hung heavily about the room. It made her nervous. She couldn't see Domenicos, but she could feel him brooding behind his paper. He was not a comfortable man.

The croissant was still warm, flaky and buttery. She had learnt to eat it the French way, without butter or jam, each bite accompanied by a sip of coffee. It was another beautiful morning. The sky was a vivid blue. The trees of the Bois moved slightly in a summer breeze. She saw some girls in jodhpurs and shirts riding along the bridle path to vanish among the trees. It was just the morning for a forest ride, the sun filtering through the green leaves and making little pools of light on the sandy paths.

'When you've finished your breakfast we must talk,' Domenicos said abruptly, and she jumped.

This was it, then. She was about to be fired. Her first experience of it, and she wasn't much looking forward to it. She had been enjoying her trip to Paris. She liked Amanda and she liked Mrs Grey. She did not like Domenicos Aegethos. Knowing the complicated family background of his life did not make his harsh aggression any more appealing. She might understand him better, but his attitude to his daughter had alienated her. Amanda deserved better than the sort of treatment he was handing out to her.

He folded his paper and looked across the table. Laura wiped her fingers and mouth on her napkin while he watched, making her feel selfconscious.

'Finished?' The question had a sardonic sound.

'Yes, thank you.'

'I've given the matter a lot of thought,' he said, without wasting any more time. 'Now that you've seen what Amanda can get up to, maybe you won't be so casual another time.'

'I wasn't casual,' she protested indignantly.

'I take your point about being unable to watch her twenty-four hours a day, but try to anticipate one of these outbreaks. And find out all about this

Pierre. She refused to answer when I asked her.'

'How surprising,' Laura muttered.

Domenicos gave her a glare. 'What's that supposed to mean?'

'What did you expect? You leapt down her throat the minute she walked in the door.'

'I'm sure you would have been sweetness and light—but then she isn't your daughter.'

'You just don't know how to handle her,' Laura told him.

'And you do?' He looked at her sarcastically, smiling rather coldly.

'I could hardly do worse than you.'

He leaned back, eyeing her, considering what she had said. 'You have a very high opinion of yourself, don't you?'

She smiled. 'Not necessarily.'

'Just a low one of me?' His eyebrows arched, amusement in his face now. When he smiled like that he looked quite different. He seemed to be two different men, in fact. Earlier last night she had met a sophisticated, rather charming man who could both listen and talk well and who could flirt without making heavy weather of it. But there was that other side to him—the violent, savage man who had emerged later. Which was the real Domenicos? Was one a mask to cover the other?

'I think you have a lot to learn,' Laura said, and he laughed aloud, his dark eyes sparkling.

'My God, do I not?'

'About your daughter,' Laura explained.

'Amanda is a female.' His smile had gone and his

face was no longer charming.

'You make that sound appalling. You mustn't condemn the whole sex because you've had some painful experiences.'

He stood up. 'What would you know about it?'

'I'm a woman.'

He looked at her derisively. 'I'd need proof of that.' Walking to the door, he said over his shoulder: 'Don't lose Amanda again. Next time I won't be so ready to forget it.'

CHAPTER FIVE

AMANDA's face wore the old sulky expression when Laura saw her later that morning. There had been no sign of her as Laura finished her breakfast, and it had seemed sensible to let her sleep. She had gone to bed so late, and, no doubt, she must have been very disturbed after that row with her father. She had probably lain awake half the night in a state of painful fury with him.

Amanda might be difficult and thorny, but she was sensitive and could be easily hurt, particularly by her father. Her feelings towards Domenicos were an explosive mixture of love and hate. Most teenagers go through a state of restless rebellion. In Amanda that state was acute.

When she did appear she stalked into the room with a glower. It amused Laura to see that she had chosen to put on one of her more violent outfits. Whenever Amanda wanted to shout defiance at her elders she put on something she hoped would infuriate them. This morning she was wearing an orange silk blouson top which left her shoulders bare and half exposed her breasts. With it she wore baggy green trousers in a virulent shade that made Laura wince, but outwardly she gave no sign of her amused revulsion, knowing that Amanda's slanting dark eyes were watching for just that sign that she had succeeded in her aims.

Unfortunately Mrs Grey was not quite so well prepared. She looked at her granddaughter's jarring clash of colours and styles and her eyes rounded in horror.

'Good morning, dear,' she said hurriedly, averting her eyes from the offending sight with great rapidity.

Amanda brushed her lips against her grandmother's cheek before turning her challenging stare towards Laura. 'Like my top?' she demanded pointblank.

'Dazzling,' Laura said.

Amanda stared, her eyes beady.

'You certainly don't intend to be missed,' Laura added.

'You hate it,' Amanda accused.

'Did I say that?'

'You think it's horrible.'

'Do I?' Laura looked at her with a little smile. 'Well, go on, what else do I think? I'm fascinated. You never told me you did a mind-reading act.'

'Ho bloody ho,' Amanda fumed, and Mrs Grey looked aghast.

'Amanda dear! That wasn't very nice.'

'Well, call off your comedian,' Amanda snapped, flinging off out of the room. 'She and my father, so-called, would make a great double act.'

Mrs Grey wrung her hands and looked helplessly at Laura. 'She's so upset!'

'I'll speak to her,' Laura promised, following Amanda out of the room with a reassuring little smile for Mrs Grey.

She found Amanda in her bedroom in her panties and bra. The offending orange top and green pants lay on the floor, and from their appearance Laura got the strong suspicion Amanda had just jumped on them.

'Can't you knock before you come in here?' demanded Amanda, swinging round, her hands on her skinny hips, bristling.

'Didn't I? Sorry, I thought I had,' Laura told her. She knew she had and so did Amanda. It was going to be one of those days.

'Come to help me choose something more suitable?' Amanda sneered, reaching down a dress which appeared to have been made out of Army camouflage material, and which was, Laura felt, very suitable in Amanda's present mood. The glitter in the dark eyes warned that it was to be war on all fronts.

Laura sat down on the edge of the bed. 'Stop giving an imitation of the poor misunderstood little orphan and listen to me . . .'

'Why should I?' Amanda slid the dress over her head and disappeared into the folds. When she reappeared she added: 'You heard the way he talked to me, the vile things he said—how would you like it?'

'I didn't understand a word. I don't speak Greek, remember.'

'Then let me interpret for you,' Amanda snarled. 'He called me a . . .'

'Don't!' Laura interrupted sharply.

'He used the word, not me!'

'Maybe he did, but that doesn't mean you have to repeat it.'

'Oh, I'm supposed to swallow it and say nothing, am I?' Amanda demanded, her lips curling.

'No, you're supposed to wait until your father is sane enough to listen to the truth and then tell him quietly and calmly that he's out of his mind if he thinks you would behave the way he suspected you had.'

Amanda stood staring at her, her face intent. 'You don't believe it?'

'Do me a favour,' said Laura, smiling.

The bitter, tense lines of the young girl's face softened. 'I thought . . .'

'Even if I'd been prepared to believe it of you, which I wasn't, I only had to take one look at Pierre to know he wasn't the type to rush you off into bed on a first date,' Laura told her.

Amanda giggled. 'Oh, no?'

Laura grinned at her. 'A second date, maybe.'

'Think so?' Amanda pretended to think about that. 'I can't wait to find out.' She sat down on the dressing table stool. 'Want to know what we really did?'

'Went dancing?'

Amanda shook her head, watching Laura with a gleam in her eyes.

'A party?'

'Nope.'

'I give up.'

'We had dinner at a café in the Latin Quarter where they play chess. Pierre's a whizz at chess. After we'd eaten we played, and he beat me hollow, then he played some games with some other guys who were there and I sat next to him and watched. One game went on for an hour and a half.'

'Grand Master stuff,' Laura commented, watching her curiously. 'Weren't you bored?'

Amanda hesitated then laughed. 'Stiff, but Pierre was enjoying himself and . . .'

'And you like Pierre,' Laura suggested, and Amanda smiled at her warmly.

'Didn't you?'

'He seemed pleasant and intelligent. I hadn't figured him for a chess Grand Master.'

Amanda smiled, then looked at her apologetically. 'Sorry I sneaked out like that—I mean, I hope I didn't drop you right in it with my father? He was so angry. I guess he went for you too, once he realised I wasn't there. I didn't mean to get you into trouble. I was horrified when I saw him there.'

'I'm sure you were,' Laura said drily.

'I knew you wouldn't let me date Pierre,' Amanda said.

'You're wrong,' Laura told her.

'I am? You would?' Amanda looked amazed, incredulous.

'It could have been arranged if you had gone about it the right way.'

'What way was that?' asked Amanda dubiously. 'You seemed dead set against him when we met him. You gave him a definite thumbs down sign from the start.'

'I was in charge of you,' Laura explained. 'I'd

given my word that you wouldn't meet anyone unsuitable or do anything your father wouldn't like.'

'So?'

'So the right way to go about things was to tell your grandmother all about Pierre and ask her if he could drop round for tea or a cup of coffee so that she could meet him,' said Laura, meeting Amanda's slanting dark eyes with a faint smile. 'Then she could have given him a grilling and found out if she approved of him, which, having met him myself, I'm sure she would have done, and you could have taken it from there.'

'What if she didn't like him?' Amanda asked, grimacing. 'And I bet she wouldn't, you know.'

'You don't have much faith either in your grandmother's judgment or Pierre's attractions if you think that.'

Amanda giggled. 'You know, you're too clever by half. You have a way of putting things that somehow manages to get past any arguments I may have thought up. Dead cunning, that's what you are. A real snake.'

'Thank you,' said Laura in a grave voice, her eyes amused. She recognised that as an intended compliment.

'And whenever I'm ready to hit you, you manage to make me laugh,' Amanda admitted, expanding on the theme. 'You just aren't fair!'

'It's an unfair world,' Laura sighed, and Amanda laughed.

'There you go again!' She sobered, giving Laura

sidelong, thoughtful looks while she chewed on her lower lip. 'Think I could start again? With Pierre, I mean? If I invited him round now do you think they'd chuck him out of the apartment block?'

Laura considered that. 'Your father might feel like it, but maybe we can get round that.'

Eager as a sparrow for crumbs, Amanda asked: 'How?'

'I'll invite him,' said Laura.

'Oh, would you really? When? Today? I've got his number here—well, his uncle's number.' Amanda flew over to her dressing table and searched hurriedly, producing a scrap of paper. 'There.'

Laura accepted it. 'Leave it with me. What's Pierre's surname?'

'Mallain,' said Amanda. 'That's spelt . . .' She spelt it slowly and Laura nodded.

'Right.'

'You're a pal,' Amanda said gratefully.

'Thank you.'

'And I am sorry,' Amanda added. 'I didn't stop to think about it from your angle—I mean, sneaking off like that.'

'I know.'

'I'm so used to them being the enemy,' explained Amanda.

It was a confused statement, but Laura understood it. 'Just remember in future—I'm not,' she said.

Amanda beamed. 'You're on my side. Great!'

Laura paused, about to correct this statement, to explain that she did not see the necessity for having sides, but Amanda looked so pleased and cheerful that she decided to leave it at that. If she managed to smooth out the field of thistles between Amanda and her father she could take a little time to get it over to Amanda that life did not have to be a battle-ground, people did not have to be put down as either friends or enemies, and Amanda was not in one lonely little army of her own with very few people fighting on her side.

Of course it looked like that to Amanda. Who could blame her for thinking that? She was still a child. She saw things in black and white.

Laura retreated and found Mrs Grey alone, staring miserably at the blue Paris sky through the window of the salon.

Laura walked towards her and Mrs Grey looked round. 'How is she?'

'Fine,' said Laura, smiling reassuringly. 'Mrs Grey, I'd like to take a little risk.'

'Oh?' Mrs Grey looked apprehensive.

'I'd like to invite Pierre and his uncle round here for a drink this evening.'

'Oh,' said Mrs Grey, with deep alarm.

'I think it would clear the air considerably if you and your son met them.'

'Oh, dear,' Mrs Grey said anxiously. 'Do you really think so?'

'It would at least get it home to Mr Aegethos that Pierre is just a pleasant teenager, not a monster.'

Mrs Grey did not seem happy with the idea. 'Perhaps we should leave well alone,' she said.

'For the sake of better future relations between Amanda and her father, I think we should have

Pierre here to meet him,' Laura insisted.

'Well——' Mrs Grey began, and Laura moved to the door.

'I'll ring him now.'

'Oh, Laura . . .'

Laura did not wait to hear the rest of that agitated sentence. She closed the door softly and went out.

She spoke to Pierre five minutes later. He was polite and friendly and accepted the invitation with alacrity.

'But I don't know if Uncle Marcel will be free this evening,' he told her. 'He works very hard at the hotel.'

'So you said, I remember.'

Pierre laughed. 'That's all he lives for.' His voice became light and teasing. 'But I'll ask him. He thought you were charming. I'm sure he will come if he can get away.'

Laura rang off, smiling. They saw nothing of Domenicos during the day. He was, Mrs Grey told her, deeply engaged in some sort of deal, the financial matter which had brought him to Paris, but he had said that he would try to get back to the apartment that evening.

'Not that that means much. Domenicos comes and goes without bothering to explain himself,' Mrs Grey sighed.

Amanda was excited, but, being Amanda, her excitement took the form of a restless refusal to admit as much. She couldn't sit still, couldn't settle to doing anything and was offhand, to say the least. Anyone who did not know her would have thought she was in one of her sulky moods. Only her constant quick glances at her watch told Laura that Amanda was on edge.

Laura could have said to her: don't be nervous, don't worry, it will work out. She knew Amanda would not listen or believe her. At sixteen every second of every hour is fraught with possibilities and threats. Amanda lived intensely in the present. No doubt in a few years' time she would find it hard to remember Pierre's name or what he looked like, but today he was the most important subject in the world, and the outcome of this evening's polite family drink with him was of vital importance to Amanda.

And anyway, thought Laura, what other way is there to live? It might seem extreme to invest so small an occasion with such importance, but was it, really? Isn't the secret of life just that—that you live for the moment, for now, and forget both past and future? Perhaps it is only in your teens that you ever really understand the secret of living. For Amanda life was a miracle, each moment bouncing along like a gaily coloured ball. Her ups and downs were a reaction to the intensity with which she met life, and Laura envied her for her ability to feel so deeply, to get so much out of life, although, of course that meant that you had as many downs as ups and suffered a good deal from time to time.

Laura had put almost all her living into work. She had barely lifted her head to look outside the hospital walls. For most of her time she had lived behind a calm, discreet mask which conferred on her the grave authority which her job required. She had realised right at the start of her nursing career that sick people trusted nurses because they wore uniforms. They did not generally see past the uniform to the worried, nervous girl inside it. From that realisation it had only been a short step to realising that your face had to wear a mask, too, a hospital uniform face which hid emotion and thought and allowed the patient to rely on you and trust you.

Gradually her face, her manner, her behaviour had become one smooth impenetrable wall—a uniform to hide Laura herself. When you spend years hiding away from those you meet it is not easy to come out from behind your wall.

Laura had only managed to do it partially for Amanda, and only then because Amanda needed help, but even then Laura had not shed any of the disguise which hid her real self. Amanda still had no notion what Laura was really like, because Amanda's intense concentration on herself and her emotional hang-ups was too great for the girl to spend any time thinking about anyone else. The egotism of the young, and of the very old, is unthinking. Laura had reached out to understand and help Amanda. She knew the girl did not really see her, had not even grasped yet that anyone else existed except as something like a cardboard cut-out on which Amanda pinned a name. She saw people only from the outside. Her father, her grandmother, Laura, were all viewed by Amanda in this simple fashion.

During adolescence there is a strong tendency to see in black and white and, always, critically. Amanda bitterly resented her father. She tolerated her grandmother. And now, it seemed, she saw Laura as her friend, her ally, one of her own kind.

That was what Laura had wanted, of course. It was a step on the way to getting Amanda to recognise that the whole world was not in a black conspiracy against her and that her life was, more or less, in her own hands. Amanda had to be helped on to a very different path before it was too late. Rebellion is a natural part of growing up, but if it becomes a way of life it can be disastrous for the rebel. Amanda could destroy herself if she stayed in her present frame of mind.

Pierre and Marcel arrived exactly on time. There was no sign of Domenicos Aegethos, but Mrs Grey, rather anxious under her polite smile, was there to greet them and Amanda was hovering around with a very offhand expression.

Mrs Grey talked to Marcel, smiling, but her eyes kept darting at Pierre. Gradually she relaxed, her smile becoming a real one. Pierre was wearing a lightweight blue suit, a shirt, a tie. He looked very neat and much younger than he had in jeans. His hair had been ruthlessly brushed down. His courtesy was only just hiding his nervous alarm at meeting Amanda's family. Mrs Grey looked at him, looked at him again, and could see that he was as innocuous as a glass of milk.

Marcel had a cynical glint of amusement as he sat down next to Laura. 'Is Pierre on display? Do you think he will pass the test?' he whispered to her, smiling at her.

'I think Mrs Grey just wanted to meet him,' Laura

evaded, smiling back.

'I understand now why you were so reluctant when we met you at Versailles,' Marcel murmured, lifting one shoulder in a little Gallic shrug. 'They are very wealthy, her family.'

Laura made no attempt to answer that. It was more of a question than a statement. Marcel was guessing from the elegance of the apartment and the diamonds Mrs Grey was wearing.

'One has to be careful,' Marcel said coolly. 'With a girl like her one has to be very careful,'

'Her family are very careful,' Laura assured him.

He nodded. 'Pierre tells me her father is Greek?'

'Yes.'

'He couldn't remember the name.' Marcel raised one dark brow interrogatively.

'Aegethos.'

Marcel's face changed. He pursed his lips in a silent whistle. 'So,' he said under his breath. 'Well, that explains it. Pierre is way out of his class, isn't he?'

Laura looked across at Pierre, who was talking to Amanda and her grandmother. They were all laughing, their faces cheerful.

Laura made no reply to Marcel's remark, but their eyes met and exchanged a wordless comprehension.

Wryly, he asked: 'And you? Are you, also, one of a wealthy family?'

Laura smiled at him. 'I'm a nurse and I have no family at all.'

His eyes narrowed. 'No family?'

'And no money,' she said, her face amused.

'I see,' Marcel murmured, obviously curious. 'You are merely a friend of the family?'

'I work for them,' Laura explained. 'I'm here to chaperone Amanda.'

'Ah!' He drew in his breath. 'It all comes clear.'

'Yes,' she said, watching his face, and wondering what was going on in his mind.

'Then will you have dinner with me one evening?' he asked, relaxing. 'I would like to get to know you better. I thought, you know, when you gave us that brush-off at Versailles, that you had taken a dislike to me, and I was sorry because I thought you were very charming and pretty.' He looked at her smilingly. 'I am relieved to realise that there was nothing personal in the brush-off.'

'I was just doing my job,' she agreed.

'Then will you have dinner with me?'

'Thank you, I'd love to,' Laura smiled.

'Tomorrow night?'

Laura considered briefly. She had not had any time off since they arrived in Paris and it had been agreed that she should have two evenings a week free.

'Yes, thank you,' she agreed.

'Can I pick you up here? At seven-thirty?'

She nodded. 'That will be fine.'

He glanced at his watch, sighing. 'I am afraid I must go. I have another appointment. I'll see you tomorrow, though.' He moved over to say goodbye to Mrs Grey, smiling down at her as he shook hands and exchanged a few polite words.

'Must you go?' she asked.

'I'm afraid so. It has been very pleasant to meet you. I hope you will allow me to entertain you one evening myself.' He did not press the invitation, but he smiled in a way which made Mrs Grey smile back with real pleasure. 'Coming, Pierre?' Marcel asked, turning to his nephew.

Pierre stood up slowly. Amanda said in a hurried voice: 'Oh, you aren't going too, are you?'

Pierre hesitated, glancing at Mrs Grey. She looked at him with a faint uncertainty, then said: 'Do stay, Pierre. You must have dinner with us.'

Amanda beamed, running her hand through his arm. 'Yes, have dinner with us.'

Marcel was watching Mrs Grey. 'Perhaps . . .' he began, and she smiled at him.

'We would love to have him,' she assured Marcel, who inclined his head gravely before leaving. Laura thought she understood Marcel's reluctance to leave his nephew with them. Marcel perfectly saw that there could be no future in that friendship and he would have preferred to stop it before Pierre got hurt. Laura understood, but disagreed. Both Pierre and Amanda were far too young for such considerations. Their friendship was unlikely to hurt either of them.

Amanda dragged Pierre off to listen to the latest hit records in her room while Mrs Grey stared after them doubtfully.

'I hope we're doing the right thing,' she said to Laura, getting up. 'I'm going to rest for an hour before dinner, my dear. I feel quite exhausted after all that.'

Laura laughed. 'I'm sure you do. It got rather

nerve-racking at times, but you did like Pierre, didn't you?'

'He seemed a perfectly charming boy,' agreed Mrs Grey. She sighed. 'I only hope Nico thinks so.'

Laura lay back on the couch, her eyes closed. She could understand Mrs Grey's mental exhaustion. She felt the same. She had taken a big risk bringing Pierre and Marcel here, but it seemed to have paid off.

'Tired?'

The voice made her spin, leaping up, her heart beginning a fierce tattoo.

Domenicos strolled towards her, smiling, his hands in his trouser pockets, his jacket open, the closely fitting waistcoat of his dark suit carrying the glitter of a gold watch-chain draped over it. His impressive height and lean build seemed a surprise to her in her dazed state. He's far too sexy and far too disturbing, Laura thought, and then was surprised at herself for thinking it.

'Hallo,' she managed to say in a husky voice, and got furious with herself for behaving like a tongue-tied schoolgirl in front of him. She knew her colour had swept up her face, her blue eyes were wide and nervous.

'All alone?' he asked softly, somehow managing to make the question very disturbing.

'Yes,' she said, struggling to control the rapid rate of her pulse.

'I hope you haven't lost Amanda again,' he mocked, his dark eyes teasing.

'Oh, I know exactly where Amanda is,' Laura told him with conscious dryness.

'And where's that?' He moved over to the de-
canters and poured himself a whisky. 'Can I get
you something? You're not a whisky drinker, I imagine.'

'I'm not,' she agreed. 'I'll have a dry Martini,
thank you.'

'Right,' he said, coming back a moment later with
the two glasses. He handed her one and sat down, his
own in his hand, looking at her over the rim of it as
he sipped the whisky.

'You look very charming,' he informed her, his
dark eyes running over the smooth frame of her pale
blonde hair and then commencing a gradual descent
over her face and figure which made her prickle with
awareness. Laura was wearing a simple black dress.
The uncluttered line of it made her look very slender,
very cool, and Domenicos followed the outline of her
body under it faithfully and with unhidden appreciation.

When his eyes came back to her face she met them
with faint frostiness.

He grinned. 'You're a very cool lady, aren't you?'

'Am I?' she asked, letting the touch of ice linger in
her voice.

'Oh, very,' he drawled. 'And you know you are.
I've never met a woman who was so much in com-
mand of herself.'

'Is that criticism or praise?' Laura enquired.

His glance mocked. 'Neither. Merely statement.'

The subject of Amanda and her whereabouts
seemed to have been dropped and Laura did not
want to bring it up again. She would have liked to

slide off, away from the dangerous proximity of Domenicos Aegethos, but she sat there, nursing her Martini and searching her mind for some pleasant and noncommittal subject to discuss, because if she left him she was afraid he might wander off and realise that Pierre was with Amanda in her room.

Laura knew that now was the time to tell him so, but somehow she couldn't face it. She did not want to see the charming, sophisticated man disappear again and face that savage barbarian who could take his place at the drop of a hat.

'What did you and Amanda do today?' he asked.

'Not much. A little shopping and sightseeing. We went to Les Invalides, but Amanda wasn't very impressed.'

'Napoleon's tomb is a horror, isn't it?' he asked, smiling.

'Very vulgar,' agreed Laura.

'But then he was, wasn't he? A little on the grandiose side,' Domenicos suggested. 'His taste ran to imperial splendour. He liked colours to be very bright and furniture to be very ornate.'

'All that Egyptian stuff,' Laura said. 'Crocodiles' heads carved on chairs and gold leaf everywhere.'

Domenicos looked amused. 'I suppose today we'd call him nouveau-riche.'

'I imagine they called him that then,' said Laura.

Domenicos looked at his empty glass and put it down. 'Why don't we have dinner out this evening?'

Laura felt her nerves jump. 'Well . . .' The invitation took her entirely by surprise and she was speechless.

He rose and looked at her with a mocking little smile. 'Scared?' he taunted.

She laughed. 'Of course not.'

'Prove it.' He extended his hand and she hesitantly put her own into it and let him hoist her to her feet. As she looked up at him the dark eyes smiled wickedly at her.

'Napoleon is such a fascinating topic. I'm sure we can find lots to say about him.'

Laura's instincts warned her that she was playing with fire if she accepted his invitation. The look in those dark eyes was distinctly personal and the likelihood was that if she went out with him she was going to be faced with the problem of how to deal with some sort of pass. Last night he had made it plain that he fancied her. It had been a delicate little pass last night. He hadn't laid a finger on her, but his dark eyes had been inviting, his voice lightly flirtatious. If she went to dinner tonight he might take it as encouragement and proceed a step farther.

While she was rapidly reviewing the situation and hesitating, Domenicos took matters into his own hands.

'I'll let them know we won't be dining here,' he said. 'Get your coat.'

'Well——' Laura said again, but she said it to his back as he walked away in that restless, energetic way. After a worried pause she followed him and got her coat. She did some rapid repairs to her appearance and joined him.

'All set?' he asked, his brows lifting as he met her eyes and saw the faint frown in them. 'There's no need to look as though I might suddenly develop fifty pairs of hands,' he told her drily. 'I'm not that crude.'

'That's a relief,' said Laura, slightly piqued, her blue eyes flashing, and Domenicos laughed as he took her arm and guided her out of the apartment.

'There's more to you than meets the eye, Laura.' His gaze swept over her again in that appraising fashion. 'And what meets the eye is very appealing.'

'Why, thank you, Mr Aegethos,' she said in a dry voice.

'Nicos,' he said.

Laura met his gaze. After a brief pause, she said: 'Nicos,' and got a warm smile which made her even more disturbed. She did not want to like Nicos Aegethos too much. She did not want to notice the sexy glint of the dark eyes or the masculinity of the long, lean body. He was far too dangerous. There couldn't be a future in it and Laura did not want to find herself with a broken heart to mend in a few weeks' time. It would be far too easy to let herself fall in love with a man as good-looking and charming as this one. Falling in love is fine. It is like drinking champagne—it sends a sparkle into the blood, makes time fly, makes you lightheaded with happiness. When you come down from that state of fizzing delight, though, you come with a bump and the hang-over you are left with by an over-indulgence in love can be very nasty. Laura did not want any hang-over. Her personal life might be slightly humdrum, but at least it wasn't painful, and she preferred things level and calm and easy to cope with.

'Live dangerously,' Nicos murmured as he put her into his black limousine a few moments later, watching her with amusement as she looked at the luxurious upholstery and fittings.

Live dangerously? Laura thought. Not me, Mr Aegethos.

CHAPTER SIX

THE restaurant at which they dined was on the ground floor of one of the most famous Paris hotels and from their table they had a floodlit view of the Place de la Concorde, which, even at this hour, was alive with traffic. Laura glanced out across the enormous open space towards the National Assembly building blocking the sky on the far side and felt a peculiar unreality in being here, alone, with Domenicos Aegethos, eating lobster delicately coated in a wine sauce and drinking champagne. It was dreamlike, unbelievable. Was it really happening to her? The thought amused her and as she turned to look at the man on the other side of the table he met her eyes and lifted one dark winged brow in enquiry.

'Something amusing you?'

'Just life,' Laura said gravely.

'You find life amusing?' Domenicos held her gaze, his dark eyes probing her own.

'Sometimes. Don't you?'

'Not particularly,' he said in a dry voice.

'Perhaps you don't give it a chance to amuse you,' she suggested, wondering what sort of man he really was behind that powerful, handsome face. She had already seen several versions of Domenicos Aegethos. How many more were there? The sophisticated charmer smiling at her now, the harsh and autocratic family man, the man who ran a large commercial empire—and how many others? All those different characters bound under one very attractive exterior—it was very disturbing.

Domenicos glanced from her smiling eyes to her warm, pink mouth. 'I'll give *you* a chance to amuse me any day,' he murmured, and she felt sudden heat running into her face.

He watched, teasing mockery in his smile, not unsatisfied to have made her blush.

'Are there any men in your life?' he asked, signalling to the waiter to refill her half empty glass.

'Hundreds,' said Laura, and got a double take.

'Hundreds?' he repeated in disbelief.

'I work in a very busy hospital.' She watched the waiter replace the bottle of champagne in the silver bucket next to their table, the ice crackling around it as it settled.

Domenicos laughed softly. 'You know what I meant.'

'I know what you meant,' she agreed, her mouth curving.

'But you prefer not to answer the question?'

'I'm not sure why you want to know,' Laura told him, sipping some of the champagne.

He leaned back in his chair, his glass of champagne in one hand, twirling it by the long stem and watching the straw-coloured liquid reflectively.

'Do I have to spell it out?'

'Yes, please,' said Laura, and got a quick, amused look. 'I have a very simple, direct mind,' she added.

'You,' Domenicos drawled, 'are a liar.'

Laura laughed. 'That's rather unkind!'

'Your mind is very far from being simple and it is
certainly not direct.' Domenicos surveyed her
through half-lowered lids, his eyes glinting through
thick dark lashes. 'In fact, I'd go farther. I'd say you
had a mind like a corkscrew.'

She frowned. 'I wouldn't say that.'

'I've had a long chat with my mother. From her
description, you handle Amanda with devious cunning.'

'Tact,' said Laura. 'That's all.'

'If you prefer to call it that,' he shrugged. 'My
mother sings your praises to the skies. I wouldn't
have taken much notice of that if I hadn't seen for
myself how cleverly you manipulate a conversation
and what a smooth operator you are.'

Laura did not much like this description of herself,
and her brows met in a frown.

He watched, eyes narrowed. 'I'm intending it as a
compliment,' he told her. 'I thought you wouldn't
be able to handle Amanda. I take it back. If you can
handle me, you can handle her.'

'I wan't planning to handle either of you,' Laura
murmured in a soft voice, and he laughed under his
breath.

'I hope you'll reconsider that, in my case.'

The waiter appeared to remove their plates while
Laura was slowly digesting that remark and finding
it very indigestible, at that. It was all light stuff at
the moment and she found it heady to sit there in the
candlelight by that window with Domenicos opposite
her murmuring flirtatiously across the table, but
tomorrow morning she might well be wishing she

had stayed firmly in the apartment where she was safe.

She had never met a man like this one, and although she was managing not to lose her cool she had a horrid suspicion that Domenicos was planning that she should lose it very definitely later this evening, and the nasty little voice at the back of her head kept warning her that there was a real danger he could get his way.

She looked at him furtively through lowered lashes and found him watching her. My God, he's *too* good-looking, she told herself sternly. Stop looking at him. It could be habit-forming and very dangerous.

They lingered over their coffee, talking about France and Paris and the places she and Amanda had seen over the last week. Domenicos knew the city intimately. He talked about it with love and familiarity. Laura listened and looked at him and told herself over and over again to stop looking. Relaxed and at his ease, he was devastating; the hard line of his mouth softened in a smile, his tanned skin smoothly shaven, his dark eyes mocking her and inviting her. He hadn't needed to spell out that invitation. They both knew it lay between them—a tacit understanding which their casual talk skated across without ever really touching. They might be discussing Paris, but that was not what their eyes were talking about, and she knew it.

On the way back to the apartment she was on edge, although she hid it under a calm smile and the occasional light remark. They found the whole place dark and silent.

'All in bed,' Domenicos pointed out, unnecessarily, as he walked into the elegant salon. 'I'm going to have a brandy. What would you like?'

Laura hesitated, biting her lip. 'I ought to get off to bed now, I think,' she said, and got a teasing sideways smile.

'Come and sit down and relax. It isn't that late.'

'Perhaps I should just check that Amanda is in her room,' she said with a sardonic little glance. 'We don't want a repetition of last night, do we?'

'Forget Amanda,' said Domenicos with a tinge of impatience. 'I have.' He turned with a glass in each hand, gesturing. 'Sit down and don't be tiresome.'

Laura shrugged and sat down, smoothing down her figure-hugging black dress while he watched with a curling smile.

'You're too thin,' he informed her.

'Sorry about that. I realise the ladies you usually have dinner with are probably rather more sexy.'

His brows rose. 'That sounds like pique.'

She laughed at herself. 'Doesn't it? Sour grapes, I'm afraid. I suppose I'd love to have a figure like Marilyn Monroe.'

'Your figure's fine as it is,' he said, offering her the glass of Cointreau. 'Thin but worth looking at.'

She sipped, knowing perfectly well that she had already had more than enough to drink and that she would be wiser not to add this glass of smooth, orange-flavoured liqueur to the champagne Domenicos had been pouring into her all evening, but suddenly in a reckless mood, no longer caring.

Domenicos had only turned on the lamp beside

the couch. The room was glowing softly around her and the glow inside her matched it. He leaned back beside her, his glass in his hand, and talked about a film he had seen the week before. Laura hadn't seen it, but she had read reviews of it and could ask him questions which kept the conversation on a fairly safe level for a while.

When he finished his brandy and put down the glass she felt rather more nervous. He leaned over and took her glass, put it down next to his, his movements studiedly casual. She knew he was going to kiss her. He knew she knew, and his dark eyes held a smiling mockery as he moved closer.

'Now, let's see just how cool you are underneath,' he murmured as his long fingers framed her face.

That question was one which had been bothering her for most of the evening. She had never been tempted by any of the men she had known in the past. Some of them had been very pleasant. Some of them had been very good-looking. None of them had ever turned her on. But she had a shattering suspicion that Domenicos was just about to do that.

She knew she ought to stop him before it went too far. She told herself she was crazy, she was taking an insane risk. She told herself to remember that he was an extremely wealthy, experienced and tough member of a world to which she was a total stranger and that whatever happened between them tonight was going to mean absolutely nothing to him but a brief amusement; while to her it could be a calamity.

Laura had always prided herself on her common sense, but she seemed to have mislaid it. She had always been calm and level-headed and sensible. Tonight she was none of those things.

She looked at that hard, handsome mocking face and knew she had to find out how it felt to be in his arms, to feel his mouth moving against her own. It might be as idiotic as jumping out of a plane without a parachute, but she was in just the right mood for doing reckless things. She had been sane all her life. Tonight she was going to be a lunatic.

His mouth was an inch away. She held her breath, a tremor running through her, and it touched her own a second later. She saw his face hazily for a fraction of time before her lids shut down. His mouth played with her lips in a slow, sensual provocation which teased her into curling closer, her arms round his neck, one hand curving over the sleek black head to press it towards her. She felt the laughter inside him, felt his mouth twitching in a broken smile, and then the softness of his kiss became fierce and urgent, and there was nothing playful or teasing in the way Domenicos drew her fully into his arms to deepen the kiss into heated passion.

She had wondered what his kiss would be like. Now she knew. It was fantastic, shattering, and she was lost, clinging to his mouth with addicted excitement, her hands moving in restless exploration of his hair, his shoulders, his long powerful back. Domenicos's fingers played with her hair, stroked her nape, deftly drew down the zip at the back of her black dress, and it never even entered Laura's head to think of protest. She felt him slide the dress down over her shoulders. Manipulating her as if she were a doll, he freed her arms, still coaxing her mouth into total surrender, then one hand tipped back her chin and he slid his mouth down her throat to press little kisses along her bare shoulders.

Eyes closed, she breathed rapidly, whimpering huskily under the onslaught of his lovemaking, her arms around his back as his head burrowed between her breasts, pushing aside the lace and silk of her black slip to kiss the warm white flesh beneath it. Laura had given up under the sensual seduction of his mouth. She didn't even know how she had come to be lying down beside him, her head on a cushion, her body half naked in his arms. Warm languor had possessed her mind and body. Pleasure and excitement locked her helpless in his experienced hands, and she didn't even try to escape.

Her shoes had gone. Her dress was gone too now; some still operating part of her mind recognised that. Domenicos's shirt was unbuttoned, his jacket discarded, and Laura was running her trembling hands over his warm, bare shoulders and the brown, muscled chest. Each caress seemed inevitable, yet each seemed surprising. She felt stupidly that he had invented them just for her. It was all new, incredible, electrifying. Why had she just discovered such devastating pleasure? She could hear Domenicos breathing harshly as she ran her fingertips over his skin. He was pressing his face into her throat, between her breasts, and his hand slid seductively against her thigh. The husky moan she gave made him raise his head to look at her, his lids down over his glittering eyes. Under her exploring hands his heart went like a steam hammer. As he looked at her she opened her own eyes and for a second they stared at each other. Her lips parted on a sigh of hunger and his head came down to take them fiercely.

Deep in the recesses of her mind Laura admitted to herself that she wasn't going to stop him, that she didn't want to, would die of frustration if he stopped.

No sooner had she faced that than she began to feel the ebb of her hectic passion. How had she got to this point? she asked herself as Domenicos kissed her, one hand softly sliding the silk slip upward over her bare thighs.

The cold little voice in her head pointed out inexorably that she had about another minute to make up her mind. They had reached the point of no return. Domenicos wasn't going to be very happy if she tried to say no now. Everything she had done, every reaction he had got from her, over the past quarter of an hour had shrieked 'yes' loud and clear. She should never have let him kiss her in the first place. That reckless impulse had led her caress by caress to this moment. She had known before she let it start that this was where he was leading her. She wasn't a child.

Domenicos suddenly lifted his head again, stiffening. 'What's the matter?'

Laura opened her eyes and looked at him warily. 'The matter?'

'You just went dead on me,' he said with impatience, his brows meeting. 'I've been kissing a statue for the last minute or so.'

Laura drew her hands down from their embrace

of his throat and pulled down her black slip, her eyes lowered. 'I'm sorry.'

'Sorry?' he repeated, his voice hardening, thickening. 'What the hell do you mean—sorry? What's wrong?'

'I can't,' she said in a thin little voice.

'Can't?' There was a silence. His hand seized her chin, lifted it so that he could look into her nervous, shifting eyes. 'Are you trying to say no?'

'I'm not trying,' Laura said, her throat dry. 'I *am* saying no, Mr Aegethos.'

His fingers hurt as they gripped her. 'Not at this late stage of the game, you don't,' he muttered, scowling blackly. 'A minute ago you were with me all the way. What happened?'

'I must have been crazy,' she said, struggling to sit up.

'You must be crazy now if you think you're turning me off like that,' he bit out with ferocity. 'I don't like cold-blooded little teases. What sort of guy do you think I am?'

He pulled her averted head round and tried to kiss her again, but she fought him, flushed and angry now, the violent grip of his fingers very painful as he pulled her towards him. In the struggle that followed they both fell off the couch suddenly. Laura dived to her feet and fled, in her slip, tearing through the darkened apartment with Domenicos running at her heels as silently as a Red Indian.

He caught her just as she got to her door. She struggled as his hands seized her waist, pushing them down. His fingers caught her shoulders to spin her round towards him and she shoved at him so violently that he staggered backwards, swearing softly under his breath. Laura dived into her room, turned the key and leaned her face on the cold wood as the adrenalin of fear drained from her. The door handle twisted uselessly. She heard Domenicos breathing on the other side. His anger and frustration came through to her in waves. He was saying something very quietly in Greek. She did not understand a single word of it, but she got the drift. He made his meaning very clear. The sheer rage in his voice was making any use of words quite unnecessary.

She heard him walk away. Slowly she turned and made her way across to the bed, her body trembling, weak at the knees.

Only when she lay there in the dark, shivering, did she admit to herself that Domenicos was not the only one suffering from frustration. She had wanted him; she had wanted him very badly. She asked herself bitterly why she had stopped him. Did it matter that he wasn't in love with her, only wanted a few hours of pleasure from her? The incredible passion she had felt came back now, briefly, in memory, and she closed her eyes and felt like screaming. Why, why had she stopped him? She had never felt like that before in her life. She might never feel like that again. Why hadn't she taken what he was offering? Given what he was demanding?

She pulled the covers over her head as though that might shut out her mind, but of course it went on working, and she could not stop it. Domenicos had been able to take her right to the edge of surrender because he knew precisely what he was doing. Those provocative, seductive fingers had years of experience with other women. Realising that devalued what they could do. Laura knew she would despise herself if she let his experienced caresses tempt her into bed with him. She had almost given way. She had wanted to do just that. But in the end the idea of such meaningless sex had disgusted her. He had been offering her a pleasure she craved for, but to him it would have been automatic, bloodless, routine, and that she could not take.

She slept briefly, woke up in the dawn light and slid out of bed. She looked out at Paris, her eyes blinking as the red sun swam up over the horizon, sending glittering reflections back from the buildings on the rim of the Bois de Boulogne. The traffic was building up again, streaming into Paris by every road. Along the shadowy paths of the forest crept the fingers of the sun, stealing between the trees and rifling the darkness.

Laura shivered and turned away. Suddenly she remembered her dress and shoes. Her face burned. She had to get them before the housekeeper spotted them.

It made her sick to see her black dress crumpled on the floor with one shoe beside it and another lying in the middle of the room. She hurriedly picked them up and retreated back to her bedroom with them.

She took a leisurely shower, got dressed and went out to have an early breakfast, her nerves very jumpy. She was afraid that she was going to have to face Domenicos now, and she couldn't imagine how he was going to treat her, after last night.

Embarrassment crawled in her skin as she walked through the apartment. She hoped it did not show on her face. But there was no sign of him at the breakfast table. She was the first one up and she drank her coffee with one eye on the brightening morning. After five minutes Amanda appeared, her face bright and sunny.

'Good morning, did you sleep well? I slept like a log all night. Oh, good, cherry jam, my favourite, much nicer than marmalade. I wonder why the English don't eat it?'

'Wrong sort of cherries,' said Laura, watching with horrified fascination as Amanda spread the dark jam thickly on her croissant. 'English cherries are eating cherries.'

Amanda bit into the croissant, her small white teeth avid. Laura looked away and drank some more coffee.

'How would you like to go to Chartres today?' asked Amanda.

'Chartres? That's rather a long way from Paris.' Laura frowned, trying to remember exactly how far away it was, but Amanda was talking excitedly.

'Pierre is going to try to persuade Marcel to drive us there. Pierre can drive, but Marcel won't let him have his car, isn't he mean?'

'Horribly mean,' Laura said drily, only too well able to imagine why Marcel refused. He no doubt had visions of his car being driven into a wall. Pierre seemed a very sensible boy, but behind the wheel of a fast car even the sanest of males goes a little crazy. It is as if the very feel of all that power in their hands excites them. Behind every grown up male there lies a little boy going: Brmm, brmm in a toy car, and the reckless love of speed which a pedal car cannot satisfy carries on into adulthood and becomes potentially fatal.

The telephone rang. Amanda rushed off to answer it, excitement in her face. When she came back she was lit up like a Christmas tree.

'Marcel says he will,' she told Laura. 'He's taking a day off and they're picking us up in an hour in front of the apartment building. We'll leave a note for my grandmother, shall we? It's too early to wake her up.'

Laura had her eyes on her coffee cup, her brow creased. 'What about your father?' she enquired as coolly as she could manage. Domenicos was not going to like this and Amanda knew it.

Amanda grimaced. 'He'll probably be working all day, if I know him. That's all he ever thinks about—work. He won't even notice we aren't here.'

'And if he does?'

'My grandmother will tell him we've gone to Chartres. He'll accept that.' Amanda grinned at her. 'He won't care, anyway, so long as you're with me.'

That was probably true, Laura thought, and if she and Amanda were out all day there would be no danger of running into Domenicos. It would put off the evil hour when she had to face him.

Amanda was staring at her, her smile going and a reproachful little frown taking its place. 'You are coming, aren't you?'

Laura smiled at her. 'Of course, I'd love to, I'm

dying to see Chartres.'

Amanda's face cleared and that sunny look came back. 'Well, I thought you would,' she said disingenuously. 'Pierre and I can wander around the town while you're looking at the cathedral with Marcel.'

Laura did not need a diagram. Amanda and Pierre had thought up this day at Chartres so that they could spend some time alone together without Amanda's family objecting. Chartres was the hook for Laura to swallow. Laura was bait for Marcel. They had very tidy minds, thought Laura, smiling. Clever, too, although they were so young. Not to mention devious and cunning.

'You're very thoughtful,' she commented, her eyes amused, and Amanda caught that expression and laughed, going a little pink.

'Yes, well,' she said, backing, 'I'll get ready.'

'I'll write a note for your grandmother,' Laura promised, watching her. She had no objection to Amanda's plan. The fact that Amanda had thought it up indicated that the younger girl had taken the point that no real hassle would start up with her family if her meetings with Pierre were carefully vetted and Laura was always around. It was much better for Amanda's relationship with Pierre to be out in the open. It took all the furtive excitement out of it and made it an approved friendship.

She wrote a careful little note for Mrs Grey, got ready and met Amanda as she came out of her room. Amanda was dancing about like a five-year-old, her face glowing with excitement.

When they met Pierre and Marcel, however,

Amanda shed that febrile excitement and was suddenly offhand and cool. 'Hi,' she said as she took the seat in the back of the car beside Pierre, and he said: 'Hi,' in very much the same way.

Marcel smiled sideways at Laura, winking. 'Make you feel very young, don't they?' he whispered, and Amanda leaned forward to demand to know what he had said.

'Nothing,' Marcel told her, starting the car. They took the congested autoroute out of Paris into the cornlands which lie between the capital and Chartres, the road winding between miles of flat fields, stretching into the distance unendingly, the blue haze of the morning mist hanging like faint smoke along the horizon.

'They used to call this the granary of France,' Marcel told Laura. 'The beautiful country—Le Beau Pays. In the Middle Ages it was always being fought over. Corn was money, and this stretch of land was worth a king's ransom.'

'It is beautiful,' Laura agreed. 'It reminds me of Cambridgeshire.'

Marcel glanced at her. 'Ah, yes, I know that part of England. Flat.'

'Very and very good arable land, just like this.'

Once they had got out of the Paris suburbs the car put on a burst of speed and ate up the long miles very rapidly. Marcel talked to her, his olive skin smooth in the sunlight, his shrewd eyes touching her face with appreciation now and then.

Suddenly he pointed. 'There—in the distance— Chartres . . . see it?'

Laura stared and her breath caught in a dazed amazement and delight. It rose out of the flat lands around it like a mirage, in the shimmering golden light, dreamlike, ethereal, the delicate spires tapering away into the blue sky, as if the cathedral lay in the cornlands like a ship becalmed. Even the strange hazy light deepened the resemblance, making one feel that the blue and gold of the morning lapped around the sides of the cathedral like pale water. It was alone, no other buildings anywhere near it, and Laura turned to ask Marcel in a hushed voice: 'Isn't there a town?'

'Of course,' he said, smiling. 'But you can't see it from here. The cathedral is built on a hill. The town is all around the hill and climbs up the side of it, too, but from here it is invisible. All we can see is Chartres itself.'

'It's the most beautiful thing I've ever seen,' said Laura, her eyes bright with unshed tears because the beauty was beyond words and only tears could express it.

Marcel smiled again, satisfied with her reaction. 'You know, there has been a cathedral on the site for centuries, but way back in the twelfth century it was burnt down, and the one we know today was built to take its place. They had no money. In those days the State didn't pay for everything.' He grinned at her. 'So the people built it themselves.'

Laura's mouth dropped open. 'That beautiful place was built by amateurs?'

Marcel laughed. 'Oh, they didn't do the actual building, no. They had the best stonemasons in

Europe for that. But they paid—little villages all over France sent whatever they could, whatever they had. They were so poor, poorer than we can understand today. But for Chartres they sacrificed their own food. Wine or wheat or sheep—whatever could be sold to raise money. It was all voluntary, you understand. It was done out of love. The rich sent money, too, but when you have a great deal of money you aren't giving so much, are you?' He crooked a wry eyebrow at her. 'It was what the poor gave that mattered, because they had so little and they gave almost all they had. They gave their time, their labour, too. Men walked for days across France just to work as labourers on the site, for nothing. All for the glory of God and love of Chartres.'

'How fantastic,' said Laura huskily. 'I had no idea.'

'Ah, well, today you see what they made in the thirteenth century with only their hands and a few stonemason's tools and a desire to make something worthy of God,' said Marcel, smiling. 'And when you look at Chartres you're no longer so very impressed with rockets to the moon. Man is an extraordinary animal.'

'What was it about Chartres that made people want to give up so much to see it rebuilt?' Laura asked, frowning. 'I mean, presumably the first cathedral wasn't as lovely as the one we have today, so why were they so determined to see it rebuilt?'

Marcel shrugged. 'There's something magical about Chartres itself, about the hill, the little town.' He gestured to the etched filigree lines of the cathedral where they faded into the morning sunlight. 'Hard to say what it is. It just exists, a very special feeling.'

When they drove into the town itself some of the incredible magic leaked out of Chartres. The huddled, grey streets were ugly and ordinary, just like those of any other small provincial town, but then Marcel turned up into a tiny, narrow winding street and Laura began to see that there were two places called Chartres—one the dull little town below the hill, the other a maze of medieval streets huddled close together as they clung to the sides of the hill on top of which the cathedral rose.

They parked next to the cathedral and all stood staring up at it in fascination.

'Wow!' exclaimed Amanda, open-mouthed. 'That's what I call a church. Look at that window!'

'The most famous rose window in the world,' Marcel told her. 'The colours are superb. Are you coming inside, you two?'

'I think we'll walk round the outside first,' Amanda said hurriedly, taking Pierre's hand. 'You go in, you two. See you later.'

It was, in fact, an hour later that they ran into them again. Marcel had taken Laura over the cathedral with the dedicated enjoyment of a fanatic, showing her every little detail. He was, he admitted to her, in love with Chartres and never bored when he was there. He had been visiting it since he was a small boy and knew a good deal about it. There was a good deal to know. Laura got the feeling that one lifetime would not be enough time in which to find out everything about Chartres. The exquisite carving, the famous stained glass, the woodwork, would each occupy the attention of one man for a lifetime.

They found Amanda and Pierre in one of the little shops arguing over the respective merits of some souvenirs. 'Hi,' said Amanda, grinning at Laura. 'Had a good time?'

'Fascinating,' Laura said. 'Did you look round the cathedral? We didn't see you.'

'I like the outside best,' Amanda said evasively.

Marcel laughed. 'Barbarian! Now, what about lunch? There are any number of restaurants here.'

They found one in a narrow street just below the cathedral and had a very good meal, the cooking superb and the service friendly. Marcel persuaded Laura to have some oysters, which she did not like, and tried to persuade her to have the famous Normandy tripe in a white wine sauce, which was also on the menu, but she stoutly refused to risk it.

'It's very good,' Amanda assured her.

'No, thank you,' said Laura. 'I'll stick to veal. You have it, if you like it so much.'

'I shall,' Amanda told her. 'You're too conservative, you British. French cooking is the best in the world. You won't get tripe like this in England.'

'No,' Laura agreed drily, and Marcel laughed, his dark eyes dancing with amusement at her expression.

After lunch they drove slowly back towards Paris, turning off the autoroute to explore the belt of countryside ringing the capital, and it was late in the afternoon before they reached the centre of the city again.

'Why don't we have a drink somewhere? It's early yet,' Amanda said, eyeing one of the little pavement cafés as they passed it on their way to the Bois de Boulogne. Everywhere you went in Paris you met them, their little white chairs occupied from early in the morning until very late at night, giving one the feeling that Paris lived outside in the street, life spilling out from the congested buildings into the equally busy roads.

'I think we'd better get back,' Laura said quietly. 'Your grandmother will worry if we're out much longer.' Not to mention your father, she thought drily. She shuddered to think what his reaction was going to be, although, with luck, as Amanda had anticipated, he would have gone off to pursue his financial obsessions and would be unaware of what they had been doing.

'You won't forget that we're having dinner tonight,' Marcel murmured to her under his breath.

He didn't speak softly enough. Out of the corner of her eye she saw Amanda grin at Pierre. 'No, I won't forget,' Laura said calmly, hoping she did not flush and cross with herself for caring what Amanda thought.

'I'll pick you up at seven-thirty.'

She nodded.

'Where I picked you up this morning?'

She nodded. 'Thank you, and thank you for our lovely day at Chartres. I'll never forget my first sight of it. It was an unforgettable experience and I'm very grateful to you for showing me something so beautiful.'

'I enjoyed it,' said Marcel. 'It is always exciting to show someone a place you love, especially when the someone is as receptive and sensitive as you are.' He glanced over his shoulder and made a face at the other two. 'Some people just don't know how to appreciate a thing of beauty.'

'That's not fair!' Amanda burst out, rising to it with youthful indignation. 'I loved it. I just hate tramping around old buildings. I liked the outside best.'

'So you said,' Marcel teased, as he drew up outside the apartment building.

'See you,' said Pierre as they got out, and Marcel gave Laura a warm smile as he drove away.

'Told you that you'd enjoy it,' Amanda said, self-congratulatingly, as they walked into the building. 'I knew Marcel fancied you.'

'Oh, did you?' Laura gave her a wry look, her blue eyes amused.

'Well, he wouldn't be dating you tonight if he didn't, would he?' Amanda asked as they walked into the lift.

'I suppose your reasoning has logic in it some-where,' Laura told her. 'It could just be that Marcel is a very polite man.'

'And it could just be that I don't believe a word of that,' Amanda retorted. 'He fancies you.'

Laura began to laugh at her expression as they walked towards the door of the Aegethos apartment. It flew open before they got to it and her laughter stopped as she looked into a pair of eyes that glittered like polished jet.

In a childlike gesture, Amanda clutched at her hand, moving closer to her for protection against the masculine aggression confronting them, but Domenicos was not even looking at his daughter. He was staring at Laura, his lip curling back from his teeth in a dangerous snarl.

'Where the hell have you been?'

CHAPTER SEVEN

LAURA lifted her chin, her blue eyes steady. 'Didn't your mother show you my note?'

'She showed it to me,' he bit out. 'It left out a few things, though, didn't it?'

Amanda's fingers tightened and Laura looked sideways at her, frowning. Domenicos in a temper was pretty alarming, but Laura had no intention of letting him see that he had frightened either of them.

'Could we discuss this inside the apartment?' she enquired, looking back at him.

His dark angry colour increased, his eyes flashed, but after a pause he stood back, and Laura walked past him, dragging a reluctant Amanda with her. The door slammed. Amanda let go of Laura's hand and shot away to the safety of her own room, scampering along like a worried mouse until she was out of sight.

Laura suppressed a little smile as she looked after the fleeing figure. She glanced at Domenicos, but he did not seem in the slightest bit amused by his daughter's hasty flight.

Domenicos seized her arm between punishing fingers and frogmarched her to the salon. The late afternoon sunlight fell across the wide room, giving an impression of light and space and grace, but there was very little grace in the way Laura was being held like a naughty little girl with those glittering black eyes glaring down at her.

'All right,' he said between his teeth. 'Where have you been?'

'Chartres—I said so in my note.'

'Your note did not mention the fact that you were going there with those two,' he snarled.

Her eyes lifted, widening.

'Yes,' Domenicos told her, his eyes hostile, 'I saw them. I watched you both get out of their car, so don't lie about it.'

'I had no intention of lying.'

'There's more than one way of lying,' Domenicos snapped in a harsh voice. 'But I've no doubt you know them all.'

Her brows drew together at the expression in his face. There was such burning, scalding rage in those dark eyes, a force of anger which was out of proportion to what had happened, what she had done. It had been the same the other night when Amanda had sneaked out of the apartment. Domenicos had erupted like a smouldering volcano into volcanic, searing fury and that indicated that beneath his usual curt manner there was hidden some sort of permanent source of anger which any small incident could tap.

'Women lie as easily as they breathe,' Domenicos said in that abrasive tone. 'It's second nature to them.'

Watching him with calm but concerned eyes, Laura said levelly: 'To put the record straight—Amanda and I went to Chartres with Pierre and Marcel Mallain.'

His eyes didn't move from her face. 'I thought I made it clear I didn't want my daughter to associate with that boy.'

'You were worried in case he was likely to be a bad influence on her,' Laura said. 'So I invited him here for a drink yesterday . . .'

'What?' he burst out.

'He met your mother,' Laura went on quietly.

'What? He *what?*' Domenicos was almost incoherent with fury, the dark colour in his face growing.

'Mrs Grey liked him,' Laura said. 'She could see that he was just as I'd described him, a pleasant ordinary boy.'

'My God, how dare you disobey my orders? I told you . . .'

'You haven't met him,' said Laura. 'If you did, I'm sure you would like him.'

'I'm damned sure I wouldn't,' he ground out.

'Then that's because you have no intention of trying,' she informed him.

'You're damned right I haven't,' he agreed.

'That's very short-sighted of you.'

'Very . . .' He was speechless.

'You can't lock Amanda up—I told you that the first day we met. This is the twentieth century and Amanda's almost grown up. In under two years she'll be of age and you won't be able to make her do anything. Why push her into an unnecessary rebellion when you could so easily make a friend of her? You're her father, her closest relative, and I think she loves you, but if you keep driving her away like this you'll end up with a stranger for a daughter.'

He moved restlessly, his frown a black bar across his forehead. 'Who are these people, anyway?'

'Marcel Mallain owns a hotel and several small businesses,' Laura said, and caught the derisive look in his eye. 'No, he isn't rich,' she said drily. 'Is that your only criterion for judging people?'

'Of course not,' he snapped. 'But even you must understand that my daughter is going to be a very wealthy woman one day and she has to be protected.'

'I understand that,' Laura agreed. 'I think you're taking it all too seriously. She likes Pierre, but at sixteen she's far too young for it to mean anything or be in any way permanent. They're friends, that's all. She may even convince herself she's in love—for a while. But she isn't, she's far too young, and far too self-obsessed. It's just one of those things.'

'Then why encourage it?' His dark eyes pinned her down, the hostility in them icy. 'For your own reasons, maybe?'

'What does that mean?' she asked wearily.

'What's your interest in the uncle, this Marcel character?'

Laura regarded him, her eyes shrewd. 'I like him. He's a very nice man. Like you, he works too hard and he's wrapped up in his business. But he also has a very romantic streak . . .'

She was thinking of Marcel's poetic reaction to Chartres, his loving fascination for the cathedral and the history behind it, but Domenicos totally misunderstood her. His eyes held a hard fixity as he stared at her and his mouth twisted in a cold sneer.

'Oh, he's very romantic, is he? I might have known you were using Amanda to further your own ends.'

Laura was suddenly angry. She stiffened, looking at him in dislike. 'I'm doing nothing of the kind!'

'Aren't you? Isn't that what all this is about? You fancy the uncle, so Amanda gets shoved into the arms of the nephew?'

'You've got a nasty mind,' she muttered.

'Lady, my mind works far too well for you to pull any fast ones on me,' he snarled.

'I'm not pulling anything. I've told you the exact truth and if you refuse to believe it, that's your problem.'

'The truth?' His mouth had a derisive indentation as he stared down at her. 'Shall I tell you what the truth is?' Laura didn't answer this, meeting his dark eyes without flinching. It was a rhetorical question because he had every intention of telling her what he thought the truth was, but Laura did not want to hear his version of it. He was going to be way off beam and she was going to find it painful to listen to him, but she knew she wasn't going to be able to stop him.

His hands came up suddenly and caught her face between them, his fingers hard and insistent as he tilted her head towards him.

'The truth is—you're a woman,' Domenicos said icily. 'And that makes you a liar, a cheat, a cold-blooded little tease who enjoys taking a man to the edge of madness and watching him fall all the way to the bottom before she walks away sweetly smiling in satisfaction.'

Laura couldn't move her head. His fingertips pressed into her cheeks, her temples, and a disturbed pulse beat under them as she watched him and saw the darkness of his eyes.

His anger had more complex roots than she could quite work out. There was a personal sense of hostility towards her, because of her rejection of him last night, but there was also the painful compressed residue of his past experience of women from his mother onwards. Domenicos did not like or trust women. He might have learned how to charm them, tease them, flirt with them, but deep down inside his mind he felt a bitter aggression towards them.

'I'm sorry about last night,' she said, and a flare of angry red stole into his face.

'Oh, I'm sure you are. I'm sure you got a great kick out of the whole charade.'

'I didn't mean to let it go so far,' Laura said unsteadily, but instead of softening him she was only making him angrier. She had chosen her words clumsily.

'So far and no farther? Is that your method?' he asked with biting rage.

'I'm not in the habit . . .' she began, and was cut off again.

'Aren't you?' he demanded, and she shook her head.

'Mr Aegethos, I realise you're angry with me.'

'Perceptive of you,' he muttered.

'But it wasn't intentional, what happened, I had no intention . . .'

'Of going all the way?' he interrupted, and she sighed.

'Don't keep putting words into my mouth.'

His dark eyes drifted down to the pink curve of her lips and she felt her beating pulse accelerate, although she wished he wouldn't stare at her like that, because she did not want to feel this strange, disturbed awareness of him.

'You asked me to look after Amanda,' she said hurriedly. 'I've honestly been trying to do just that. You may not approve of my methods . . .'

'I don't,' he said, without his eyes leaving her lips, and she could almost have sworn she could feel their stare, a hot imprint that made her skin glow.

'I asked you to trust me,' Laura said.

'I've never trusted a woman in my life,' he told her, lifting his black head and looking into her eyes, a grim smile hovering around his mouth. The pupils of his eyes were dilated, far larger than normal, giving his stare a brilliance which bothered her.

She struggled to talk normally, to think clearly. 'If you don't want to make an enemy of Amanda, you've got to trust her, let her feel free.'

'Free to make a fool of herself?' he demanded impatiently, and Laura smiled at him with faint pleading.

'I'm afraid so.'

His mouth hardened and he shook his head at her. 'No way.'

Laura gave a little sigh. 'Mr Aegethos, believe me, there's no other way. Nobody learns from other people's mistakes. We only learn from our own.'

He grimaced. 'She's too young to be allowed to make mistakes.'

'They're the only mistakes she's ever going to believe in,' Laura said gently. 'She won't listen to yours.' Their eyes met and he had a faintly surprised expression. 'If you made any,' Laura said gravely, her eyes softly teasing him. 'I'm sure you didn't.'

'Oh, are you?' he asked wryly.

'But whatever they were, Amanda won't think they have any lesson for her. If you tried to tell her she'd start laughing at you. She won't listen. All she knows is now, what's happening to *her*, and however it may infuriate you, you're going to have to let her find out for herself what life is like.'

He released her and walked away with a restless, prowling gait, his hands in his pockets and his black head bent. Laura watched him, waiting, wondering what was going on inside that odd mind of his.

Swinging, he said: 'I'd better have a look at him myself.'

She smiled. 'Good idea.'

His glance was sardonic. 'I thought you'd like it. Let me point out, however, that that does not automatically mean that I approve of my daughter having dates with a boy. She's far too young, in my opinion.'

'Of course she is,' agreed Laura.

'Then why do you encourage it?'

'You can't shut the stable door after the horse has bolted,' Laura said, shrugging. 'Amanda thinks she's grown up. You won't convince her that she isn't, at this late stage.'

'Try looking at it from my viewpoint,' he said flatly. 'She's my daughter, I'm responsible for her. I don't want her making a mess of her life before she knows what she's doing.'

'I understand that, and if we keep a watching brief I'm sure we can steer her in the right direction without too much hassle, but it will take a lot of patience and a lot of tact.'

He eyed her consideringly. 'And you've got both?'

Laura didn't answer, but her blue eyes held a smile.

'I could put another name to it,' he said mockingly. 'I'd say you have a very large share of female cunning.'

'Thank you,' she said with a grave expression.

He laughed, but then the smile went out of the dark eyes. 'But don't imagine for a moment that I've forgotten the way you ran out on me last night, because I haven't,' he told her with abrupt force, and Laura almost jumped back in shock at the look in his face.

He watched the nervous flicker pass over her features and a curious, tight little smile pulled at his mouth. 'I never forget a debt, and you owe me something now,' he told her.

'I don't owe you anything!' Laura broke out, disturbed and shaken. 'I'm sorry if I misled you . . .'

'You didn't mislead me,' he said harshly. 'You knew what you were doing.'

'No!'

'Oh, yes,' he contradicted. 'You were leading me deliberately, right up the garden path. I'm certain about that. The only thing I'm not sure about is why. There could be several reasons—you might be the type who likes a prolonged chase before she gives in, or on the other hand you might be the type who never means to give in at all, but likes to see a man going crazy.'

Laura was stiff with indignation as she listened. 'And I might be the type to slap your head off if you talk to me like that!' she told him furiously, her hands clenching.

He moved with whip-like speed, his fingers closing round her slender wrists like steel cord and pulling her arms back behind her so that she was helpless, struggling vainly as he moved so close that their bodies touched. Her breathing stopped for a beat of time before it began again much faster, her eyes widening in shock and anger.

'Don't think I'd give you the chance,' he mocked, smiling as she stopped twisting in his hard grip. 'And whatever you do, don't underestimate me, Miss Crawford. I've forgotten more about women than most men ever find out. I'm far too experienced to let a woman make a fool of me and get away with it. As I said, I don't know if you were trying to get me very interested so that I'd keep chasing you or if you were just getting a kick out of tormenting me—but I promise you, I have every intention of finding out.'

Her skin was burning as she felt the glittering challenge of those eyes running over her upturned face. The taut pressure of his lean body against the helpless curve of her own made her nervously angry, and she said shakily: 'Let go of me, please. You're making me very angry.'

That amused him. His dark eyes gleamed with laughter. 'I'm shaking in my shoes,' he whispered, mouth curling up at the edges. He jerked her arms into the small of her back, using them as a lever to force her even closer, so that his powerful chest was crushed again her breasts, his muscled thighs brushing her legs. 'Now what are you going to do to me?' he asked teasingly, and Laura glared at him in impotent fury.

'Is that supposed to demonstrate that you're stronger than I am? Well, big deal, but what does that prove? It certainly doesn't make me like you any more. Does it do your ego good to manhandle me and show me that in a straight fight I'd lose to you? That's the only reason you're so furious about what happened last night, isn't it? I hurt your ego when I said no. Well, I'm sorry. I certainly didn't intend to do that. I realise I touched on a nerve, but I'm afraid both your theories about me are way off course. I'm not inviting you to chase me, Mr Aegethos, nor was I trying to torment you. I've told you the absolute truth. One thing led to another last night without my intending any of it, and I'm sorry, but as far as I'm concerned I'd rather we forgot the whole incident.'

Domenicos listened, his dark eyes smouldering as he watched her, his brows jerking together as her torrent of fast, angry words poured out. When she breathlessly came to a stop he went on staring for a moment while Laura felt her face growing hotter and her pulse rate going faster than the speed of light.

'Well, well,' he said softly after a while. 'The lady's not so cool after all.'

The amusement in his face was real and Laura felt herself relaxing, a rueful smile pulling at her mouth.

'Sorry,' she said, 'I lost my temper, and I don't often do that. I'm afraid you provoked me, Mr Aegethos.'

'Then that was tit for tat,' he said. 'Because you certainly provoked me.'

'I didn't intend to,' she insisted.

He shrugged, releasing her at last and moving away. 'You're an interesting mixture, Miss Crawford. On the outside you're very collected, very together, but there's a lot going on inside that calm face, isn't there?' There was assessing intelligence in his eyes. 'I've got a sinking suspicion that you're that rare phenomenon, an honest woman, which would make you almost unique. I didn't think I'd ever meet one any more than I expect to find the abominable snowman in my garden.'

'Life's full of surprises,' said Laura, smiling, her colour much more normal now.

'Isn't it?' He smiled back at her. 'Give me Pierre's telephone number, if you've got it, and I'll ring him and invite him over for a drink.'

Laura wrote it down and handed it to him, watching him as he walked to the phone.

'I'll ask his uncle along too,' he said with his back to her.

'He's taking me out to dinner this evening,' Laura

said without thinking, and the black head jerked round towards her, Domenicos's eyes sharply narrowed.

He made no comment, however, and Laura walked to the door on slightly unsteady legs as he dialled.

She found Amanda sitting on her bed, cross-legged, her feet bare, her black hair glossily brushed around her pale face. As she saw Laura she broke out: 'What did he say? What happened?'

'Quite a lot,' Laura said drily.

'Was he mad?'

'As blazes.'

Amanda groaned. 'He isn't going to put his foot down and try to stop me seeing Pierre?'

'Would you, if he did?' Laura asked curiously, taking off her dress.

'Not likely,' said Amanda, bristling at once. 'He couldn't make me, wild horses wouldn't make me.'

Laura smiled, flicking along the row of clothes in the wardrobe as she tried to make up her mind what to wear.

'Fortunately you won't have to make the choice. He's just ringing Pierre to invite him round.'

'You're kidding!' Amanda sat up on her knees, her face excited.

'No,' Laura said.

Amanda leapt off the bed and hugged her. 'Magic, you're miraculous, how did you do it?'

'Your father isn't quite as unreasonable as you believe,' Laura said, crossing her fingers behind her back.

'He isn't?' Amanda didn't sound convinced, which wasn't so surprising when you remembered the barbaric fury in Domenicos's face as they arrived earlier. A cynical look crossed the small, sallow face. 'This must be one of his good days, then.'

'He worries about you,' Laura told her.

'A bit late in the day.' Amanda set her small pink mouth stubbornly. 'He never has before. Why should he start now?'

'Perhaps you never understood him before,' Laura suggested. 'You were only a child then. Now that you're grown up you're beginning to see him more clearly.'

Amanda stared at her. 'Am I? I think I saw him pretty clearly before. All he thinks about is work. He's never cared what happened to me.'

'He cared,' Laura said gently. 'It isn't always easy to show you care, and he is a very busy man.'

'Too busy to bother about me,' corrected Amanda, walking to the door, flicking back her sleek hair with an impatient hand as she left the room.

Laura sighed. Amanda was still partially a child. She wasn't yet set in any particular mould. Her moods, her tantrums, her flaring defiance and rebellion, were like the clouds which pass over the blue sky in spring: fleeting, temporary, masking the possibility of finer weather. At the moment she was poised between two worlds—childhood and adulthood. She could be anything. She could move in any direction. At the moment it was impossible to say what sort of person Amanda really was, but it was absolutely essential that those clouds should roll away, not gather thicker and faster until they totally obscured the sunlight from her.

It could so easily happen. It had happened to her father. His life had been darkened when he was young by his mother's desertion, his father's early death. He had grown up full of resentment, hostility and disillusioned dislike towards women. Family relationships not only form the mind of a child, they make the basis for all the relationships which come after them. Laura could imagine that for a man with a strong mind and an even stronger will it would be all too easy for such deeply embedded emotions to dominate the pattern of later life.

She stripped off the rest of her clothes and took a shower. As she stood in the warm water, feeling the tingle of the fine spray hitting her naked skin, she warned herself of the dangers of getting any more involved with the Aegethos family. The web was too tangled, the human relationships between the three of them too broken and piercing. Anyone who stepped into that triangle was likely to get hurt, and Laura's common sense told her to stay out of it.

She had taken this job to tide herself over until she could go back to her real world, the life she had built up for herself. If she had any sense she would remember that this was a brief excursion into a world where she did not belong. She was already emotionally involved with Amanda and Mrs Grey, her feelings for both of them were warm and concerned. But they weren't as dangerous as Domenicos. He was an adult. Let him work out his chaotic family relations for himself.

The pleated white dress she wore swirled around her slim legs as she halted, a quarter of an hour later, her eyes flying across the salon. Domenicos stood at the window staring out over the Paris night sky, but he turned to survey her as he heard her. A glass of whisky in his hand, he stood there casually in an evening suit, the golden tan of his skin shown up by the crisp white of his shirt, his powerful muscled shoulders straining under the smooth jacket, and let his narrowed gaze drift down over her.

Laura felt the bloom of hot colour crawl into her face under that insolent, mocking appraisal. She was furious with herself. She had had years of training to teach her how to keep her cool, keep out of sight her reaction to what was happening around her. She did not like admitting to herself that the sensual slide of Domenicos's eyes sent a jungle drum beat through her veins and made her skin prickle with heated awareness.

'Drink?' he murmured huskily after a moment.

'Thank you.'

Their eyes disengaged and Laura slowly walked over to sit down, crossing her long legs while Domenicos watched. He moved over to pour her a drink.

'Dry Martini, isn't it?'

She nodded. 'Thank you.'

'Ice? Lemon?'

'Thank you.'

He moved over to hand her the glass and she felt her pulses start up again as his cool fingers touched her own.

He didn't sit down but stood watching her, his

glass in his hand, sipping the whisky from time to time while he surveyed her over the rim of his glass.

'You told Amanda?'

She nodded, smiling.

'Delighted, was she?' Sarcasm tinged his face.

'I think you could say that,' Laura agreed, amused.

'Hmm,' he said, a shrewd flicker of answering amusement in his stare. 'I hope he isn't going to take it for some sort of tacit approval on my part.'

'I'm sure he's shivering in his shoes, right now,' Laura told him with faint mockery, and he ran his eyes from her smiling blue gaze to the pale golden frame of her hair as it curved around her face.

'I could get addicted to that,' he murmured, and Laura looked at him in bewilderment.

'What?'

'The way you smile,' he said, and watched the little tide of pink colour rise in her face.

Looking away, she said: 'I'm sure you're going to like Pierre. There's nothing to dislike.'

'Oh, I've got my orders, have I? I like him or else?'

'Nothing of the kind, just meet him with an open mind.'

'That's more than Amanda does with my friends,' Domenicos said. 'Especially the female ones—she usually detests them.'

'Does she?' Laura thought about that, her brow wrinkling. 'Jealousy, I suppose. It wouldn't be surprising.'

'I couldn't say,' he told her curtly.

The door bell rang. He put down his glass and moved towards the front door as the housekeeper answered the polite little ring. Laura sat with her glass in her hand, listening as Domenicos spoke quietly, politely, rather distantly.

Pierre wore a worried, alarmed smile, his pleading dark eyes apprehensive. He gave Laura a jerky little nod and said: 'Good evening.'

Marcel calmly came round to sit down next to her, giving her a glinting and cynical little smile. He obviously understood quite well what was happening.

Domenicos poured a drink for each of them and as they were accepting them Amanda rushed into the room, pink and glowing and excited. She stopped as she saw her father, and Laura watched the nervous look she gave him. Domenicos surveyed her without speaking and Amanda's mouth drooped, the old sullen look coming back. When Amanda scowled like that she could look quite plain, her sallow skin and dark eyes emphasising the slender body and small face. It was only in motion that her features could take on a lively warmth, an engaging excitement which altered her whole appearance.

'What did you think of Chartres?' Domenicos asked her, pouring her a glass of orange spiked with a tiny dash of gin.

Amanda took the glass, her fingers far too tight as they held it. 'Lovely,' she said, still wary.

Domenicos studied her drily, then looked at Pierre. 'Have you been there before, or was this your first visit too?'

'I've been there before,' Pierre said nervously, sitting on the edge of his chair. He looked, thought Laura, about twelve, in his very neat suit and carefully tied tie. Even Domenicos couldn't imagine the boy was a dangerous influence for Amanda. If anything, Amanda was likely to be a dangerous influence for Pierre. 'It's great,' Pierre added with slightly dubious enthusiasm.

'Especially outside,' Marcel drawled sarcastically, and his nephew looked daggers at him.

'Outside?' asked Domenicos, his brows meeting.

'They didn't go in,' Marcel said, amused.

Domenicos glanced at Amanda, who had gone even more pink. She looked at Marcel, her slanting dark eyes aggressive.

'We had a good look at all the stained glass and the spires, and the carving on the doors is fantastic.'

'I was fascinated by the stained glass,' Laura interrupted, and began to talk about the things she remembered most vividly, deliberately taking some time in listing them, so that attention was taken off Amanda's sullen face.

'But what I shall remember most is seeing the cathedral as we drove towards it,' she added. 'That was really something.'

'It is quite a sight,' Marcel smiled at her. She smiled back before glancing at Domenicos. His face was unreadable, but somehow she felt uncomfortable as she glanced away again.

'I gather your parents are on holiday?' Domenicos asked Pierre, who nodded.

'In Algiers,' Pierre said.

'How long will they be away?'

'Three weeks,' said Pierre.

'And they left you behind?' The black brows winged upwards in mock surprise.

'I didn't want to go,' Pierre explained. 'I shall be going away on a camping holiday with friends later in the summer. I prefer to take my holidays alone these days.' His tone was consciously adult and Laura suppressed a little smile.

'Great idea,' said Amanda, her dark eyes daring her father to comment.

'Isn't it?' Domenicos murmured, eyeing her with sarcasm. 'And you're staying with your uncle?' he asked Pierre, looking back at him.

He nodded, and Marcel watched, smiling. Domenicos slowly turned his head to view him thoughtfully.

'I'm told you are in the hotel business?'

Marcel agreed drily that he was.

'I have some hotels myself,' Domenicos said, and Marcel answered even more drily that he was aware of that, naming one very famous hotel in Paris.

'Out of my class, I'm afraid,' he said.

Domenicos smiled tightly. 'It is a very good hotel.'

Marcel glanced at his watch, then gave Laura a faintly conspiratorial smile. 'If we are going to have dinner, I'm afraid we shall have to be leaving now,' he said, and she stood up, placing her glass on the small leather-topped coffee table.

Pierre got up too, uncertainly, his face very flushed, and Domenicos looked at him with enigmatic eyes.

'Won't you stay to dinner with Amanda and myself?' he asked with every appearance of courtesy.

Pierre looked uneasy, but Amanda grabbed his hand and jerked him back into his chair.

'He'd love to,' she said with confidence.

Laura and Marcel walked to the door and Domenicos accompanied them like a guard dog, his manner containing sufficient bristling hostility for Marcel to say to Laura under his breath: 'I think I'm being seen off the premises.'

Domenicos did not catch the remark, but he knew a remark had been whispered and his scowl was very alarming as he opened the door for them.

Laura glanced up sideways at him and got a glower that made her do a double-take.

'Don't be late,' said Domenicos, then he let the door slam, whether intentionally or not she couldn't be sure.

Marcel whistled under his breath. 'He does not like me,' he said. 'Odd, that—I can understand his being doubtful about Pierre, but why did I get looks like knives?'

'You're Pierre's uncle,' Laura suggested.

'And he's suspicious of anyone prowling around his daughter?' Marcel shrugged. 'You're probably right. I see his point. She's an heiress and very young—I'd take exactly the same attitude if I was her father.'

'Would you?' asked Laura in surprise.

'Of course,' said Marcel, even more surprised than Laura had been. 'It would be so easy for someone unscrupulous to run off with her. See how easily

Pierre got into talk with her. She's very innocent and trusting.' He smiled at Laura. 'And so are you, or you wouldn't have let it happen.'

'I tried to stop it,' Laura said.

'So you did, but not in a determined way.'

'You didn't look very dangerous to me,' Laura told him, and he laughed.

'Thank you, I hope that's meant as a compliment, although no man enjoys being told he doesn't look dangerous.'

'Oh, do you want to look dangerous, then?'

'It would be flattering to the ego,' Marcel admitted, his attractive face full of teasing. 'I suppose inside most men there is a Don Juan lurking only waiting for a chance to get out.'

'I've never thought much of Don Juan, a rather boring fellow, in my opinion. He isn't a romantic hero, at all. He hasn't any feelings and the hero has to have feelings if he is to be really romantic.'

'Mozart gives him some ravishing music, feelings or no,' said Marcel, and they plunged into discussion of Mozart that managed to occupy their attention for most of the rest of the evening.

'I thought we would go Bohemian tonight,' Marcel told her in his car. 'We're dining in the Latin Quarter.'

'That sounds lovely,' she told him eagerly.

'The food is quite good, the surroundings fascinating and the other guests are likely to be a colourful collection,' he said, smiling. 'It will give you a new view of Paris.'

By the time they actually reached the little restaurant Laura was very flushed, rather indignant and ached from the pinches she had received en route. The narrow dirty streets were packed with people. Every second male she passed gave her a come-hither smile and murmured inviting words in some language or another. A lot of them were foreign, Algerians, Germans, Swedes, but they did not need to speak English in order to get over what they were saying. In case she didn't get the point they touched her admiringly, laughing when she slapped their hands away.

'Sorry,' said Marcel, grinning. He always managed to drive them off with a growled word or two, but there were so many of them and they swarmed like bees around honey as soon as they saw Laura's blonde hair and slim, curvy figure. 'You are paying the price for being so delightful, I'm afraid,' he teased. 'Do you want me to punch the next one in the nose?'

'Don't bother,' Laura said, groaning as another group of young men leered at her. '*Allez-vous-en!*' she spat, and they laughed and walked on.

'Very impressive,' Marcel laughed. 'You're picking it up well.'

'That was what you kept saying to them, wasn't it?' she asked.

'That was it, and you'll find it a handy phrase.' He dived into a dark little opening. 'Here we are . . .'

Laura looked around the shadowy interior. Stubs of candles flickered on the crowded tables. A guitarist strummed noisily in a corner. Faces peered, voices muttered.

'Do you like it?' Marcel asked, amused.

'It's . . . charming,' said Laura, and he laughed.

'There's one thing about it,' he told her. 'It's too dark to see what you're eating, which may be just as well. As long as it tastes fine what does it matter what it looks like?'

The food was brought to them on enormous wooden platters, and Laura knew she was not going to be able to eat so much as half of the great piles of roast meat, salad, rice and potatoes baked in their jackets. The menu was vaguely Greek, but it had somehow suffered a sea change on the way to Paris and was neither one thing nor the other. It was, however, very edible, and the atmosphere in the little restaurant made the meal a gay, colourful occasion.

Afterwards she and Marcel walked through the Latin Quarter again towards Notre Dame, dropping into the English bookshop near the Seine to look along the crowded shelves before walking down to the river.

'Why do they call it Shakespeare and Company?' Laura asked as they left the bookshop.

'I suppose as a joke,' said Marcel. 'They sell only English books. It is famous, this place. Henry Miller praised it to the skies.'

'They stay open very late,' Laura commented, looking at her watch.

'Tourists flock there in the evenings,' Marcel told her, pausing to look from the bridge on which they now stood down to the oily dark waters of the Seine. There were people sitting on the embankment on either side of the river. A boat slowly slid under the bridge, its lights leaving flickering yellow lozenges on the surface of the water, the voice of the guide coming up faintly to them, in broken disjointed English and then in crisp gunfire French.

The air was warm and soft although it was so late. They walked on towards the stern façade of Notre Dame, whose rows of archaic regal faces stared down indifferently at the sprawling life beneath them.

In front of the cathedral there was a constant ebb and flow of noisy activity. People wandered about talking. Others sang, grouped around a young man with a beard and grubby jeans playing a guitar. A small crowd watched the boneless movements of a white-faced mime in a black bowler hat and black leotard. Some children were playing with a ball and here and there lovers sat kissing, their arms around each other. Laura looked around her, smiling. It seemed to her that Paris lived out in her streets, as if each day was an enormous party, a spontaneous coming together which did not take account of time or place and which was quite unlike the more conventional behaviour you were likely to find around the great public buildings of London. Laura tried to imagine St Paul's surrounded by such uninhibited life, but couldn't.

'I love Paris,' she said, turning to Marcel with bright eyes, and they smiled at each other.

CHAPTER EIGHT

IF they had ended the evening there, all would have been well, but as they wandered along the bank of the Seine they heard the sound of jazz in a street café and Marcel suggested: 'Shall we have a last drink?' Laura hesitated. He grabbed her hand and yanked her back across the street, weaving through the rows of cars making their way along the Rive Gauche. The café was crowded, the music lively and exciting. It wasn't until Laura accidentally caught sight of her watch that she gave a groan of horror. 'It's two o'clock!'

'Is it?' Marcel seemed unconcerned, then he looked into her worried eyes and asked: 'What's wrong?'

'I haven't got a key,' Laura muttered, facing the fact that she had a serious problem. Why had she let the time drift by like that? What was she going to do? 'Everyone will be in bed by now,' she said. 'I'd have to wake someone up.' She grimaced to herself. 'If I ring the door bell I'll wake everyone up!' The thought of the reaction she was likely to get from Domenicos made her blood run cold. He was going to be furious.

Marcel took her upper arm, his hand confident. 'The problem is easily solved. You'll spend the night with us.'

Laura couldn't help giving him a quick, faintly

wary look, and he grinned at her.

'No need to look at me like that. Pierre is living with me at the moment, remember. You won't find yourself alone in an apartment with a sex maniac.' His dark, cynical eyes glinted down at her and she relaxed, smiling back.

For a moment she hesitated, realising that he was right. It would certainly solve the immediate problem. But she had a shrewd idea that if she did stay out all night with Marcel she would be creating further problems the moment Domenicos realised she had not come back but had spent the night at Marcel's apartment. Laura might be perfectly safe with Marcel; she might know that, but Domenicos was going to leap at once to the worst conclusions, and although Laura told herself she didn't care what he thought she knew she would hate to have him think the worst of her.

She shook her head reluctantly. 'Thank you, Marcel. It's very kind of you, but I think I should go back to the apartment and risk having my head bitten off by Mr Aegethos.'

Marcel eyed her with wry tolerance. 'As you like. It's your funeral.'

'Don't say that,' protested Laura, laughing. 'I've got a horrible suspicion it may be all too accurate a prediction.'

'Then why risk it?' he asked, not unnaturally.

'It could be worse if I don't,' Laura explained, and Marcel grimaced.

As they were driving back to the apartment he suddenly exclaimed: 'The concierge!'

'What?' Laura queried, puzzled.

'She must have a key, of course. Why didn't I think of that before?'

'Of course she must,' Laura said slowly. The concierge of the apartment block had a small apartment on the ground floor and beadily watched all the comings and goings of the other tenants as well as keeping the corridors and lifts clean. 'But I expect she'll be asleep too.'

'Oh, I've no doubt,' said Marcel, amused. 'But we'll get round that,' he added slightly cynically.

The concierge was irate when she finally opened her door. She was a short dark woman with a belligerent face and her hair in small metal curlers. Dragging her dressing-gown together with one hand, she peered at them crossly. 'What do you want?' she demanded in French. 'What do you mean, waking me up at this hour . . .' Her voice cut off as Marcel waved a large bank note under her nose. She watched it wave to and fro for a second, then looked at him, narrow-eyed. 'Yes, *m'sieur*?' she asked less angrily.

He explained the situation, and the concierge eyed Laura closely. 'Ah, yes, you are staying with Madame Grey,' she agreed. 'Wait here.' She shuffled away in her old carpet slippers and came back a moment later with a key in her hand. 'I will let you into the apartment myself, *mademoiselle*.'

Marcel came up with them in the lift. The concierge yawned several times, flapping a hand in front of her mouth. 'You woke me up. I have a long day, you know,' she said, and Marcel smiled at her soothingly.

'Yours is a hard job.'

'It is,' she agreed, nodding. 'People don't realise all the work I have to do. I don't get any thanks. On my knees from morning till night, scrubbing away, but nobody notices. They expect the place to be clean. They don't ask who keeps it clean . . .'

Laura was feeling flat and sleepy. The woman's sharp voice went on beside her and Marcel made soothing noises whenever there was a pause. When they reached the apartment, the concierge unlocked the door. '*Et voilà*,' she congratulated herself, nodding to them. Marcel presented her with the money. She wished them goodnight and shuffled away on her flat feet.

Marcel looked down at Laura, smiling. 'There, you see? Easy, wasn't it?'

'Thank you, I'm very grateful,' said Laura, smiling and offering him her hand. She hoped he would not try to kiss her. She liked him and had had a wonderful evening, but she did not want him to get the wrong idea. 'Thanks for a lovely evening.'

He looked at her drily, took her hand and brushed his lips against it. 'Goodnight, Laura,' he said, and his cynical eyes told her that he perfectly understood how she felt.

She slid into the apartment and closed the door. The rooms were dark. Tiptoeing, Laura began to creep along towards her own room, when a light suddenly flashed on, making her jump in alarm. She whirled round, a hand at her mouth, and Domenicos was leaning on the doorframe of the salon, his arms folded and a harsh frown across his forehead.

'Oh!' Laura exclaimed, startled.

'What time do you call this?' His voice had a deep, cold timbre. His eyes were icy.

'We forgot the time,' she mumbled, flushing.

The hostile eyes ran over her, taking in the wind-blown dishevelled hair, the flush, the nervous expression, and involuntarily, Laura shivered, seeing herself through his eyes for a brief instant and embarrassed by what she knew perfectly well was in his mind.

'Enjoying yourself, were you?'

'Yes,' she said defiantly, because she had done nothing wrong, and even if she had he had no right to look at her with that contemptuous, dismissive coldness. But he was her employer and she felt impelled to add: 'I'm sorry I'm so late. I hope you weren't waiting up for me.' He was fully dressed, but the light had been off and she wondered what he had been doing sitting in the salon in the dark at this time of the night.

'I was,' he said shortly. 'Come in here—I want to talk to you.'

She hesitated. 'It's very late,' she reminded him, and he turned on her, his teeth bared.

'I'm aware of that.'

'Couldn't it wait until morning?'

'No, it could not,' he said tersely. He turned and strode back into the salon and after a moment she followed him, so nervous she was trembling. The room was immaculately tidy except that beside one chair stood a small occasional table and on it stood a half-drunk glass of whisky and the whisky bottle. Domenicos went over, picked up the glass and swallowed the contents, his black head flung back, then he slammed down the glass with a crash that made her jump and turned on her, his face dangerous.

'All right, what do you think you're doing, coming in at this hour and disturbing the concierge to let you in?'

'I'm sorry——' she began, flustered, and he cut her short.

'I'm sure you are. Sorry I was up and realised what was going on! I had half a mind to come out and tear several strips off Mallain, but I wasn't making a scene out there with that nosy bitch of a concierge in earshot.'

Laura bit her lip. 'I'm grateful you didn't,' she said, horrified at the idea of what would have happend. 'I apologise if I caused you to wait up for me, but I'm quite capable of looking after myself, you know.'

'While you're living under my roof I'm responsible for you,' he bit out.

'I appreciate the attitude of concern,' she said with faint sarcasm. 'But forgive me if I say that I'm responsible for myself, Mr Aegethos. The only person you're responsible for around here is Amanda.'

He prowled towards her, his dark eyes accusing. 'Is that some sort of challenge? Do you think I don't know what goes on inside that head of yours? Ever since the day you walked into my office and looked at me with those critical blue eyes you've made it quite plain you think I'm no sort of father.'

Laura looked back at him calmly, saying nothing. It seemed to infuriate him even more.

'What gives you the right to sit in judgment on me?' he demanded forcefully, his features grim.

'What gives you the right to shout at me because I stay out until two in the morning with a friend?' Laura asked sweetly, and his brows met in a jagged black line.

'That's different.'

'Of course, it would be.'

'And don't be clever,' he snapped. 'You're living under my roof and you're a woman alone in a strange city. I've every right to make sure you're safe. What sort of employer would I be if I didn't?'

'Is it part of your role as my employer to check on my comings and goings?' she enquired.

He stared at her, his face furious and indecisive, as though not quite sure how to answer, then he pushed his hands into his pockets and rocked on his heels in an impatient way.

'God knows why, but I was anxious,' he muttered after a moment, and Laura looked at him in surprise and disbelief. A faint redness stole into his face under her stare and he burst out: 'Take a look in a mirror some time. You've been shut up safely inside a hospital ever since you left school. Do you think it doesn't show? You've got the face of a nun; cool and calm and as tranquil as a glass of water. Your experience of men is below zero, I'd say. Oh, I've no doubt you're a clever girl and very good at your job, but apart from that you're a prim little virgin.'

Scarlet swept up her face. She drew a shaken breath and looked away. She heard him laugh angrily.

'You are, aren't you? It's the only way I can make you add up. When I tried to make love to you the other night you ran out on me because I'd scared you rigid, and there could be only one reason for that if you weren't acting in a calculated way.'

Huskily, she said: 'I thought you believed I was.'

Domenicos gave a short sigh. 'Yes—I'm sorry, it was a rotten thing to say and I didn't really believe it. I was in a temper.'

'I remember,' she said drily, her eyes flickering back to his face.

'When I'd cooled down I regretted it.'

Laura smiled at him. 'Apology accepted,' she said in a light voice. 'And I was perfectly safe with Marcel, you know. He's a very nice man.'

Domenicos made a little grimace. 'You're too damned innocent to know, that's the trouble.'

'Oh, no,' Laura said coolly. 'I've worked with too many men not to know a man on the make when I see one, despite what you think you read in my face. I know every technique men use. I've heard all the corny old lines. Do you honestly think that being a doctor makes a man sexless? On the contrary, Mr Aegethos, doctors can be all too human.'

He stared at her, his dark eyes brooding. 'But I was right about you, wasn't I?'

For a few seconds she was bewildered, staring into his eyes, then she realised what he meant and her colour came sweeping back, her gaze hurriedly shifting away from him. She didn't answer. Did he really expect an answer to that question?

Turning towards the door, she said huskily:

'Goodnight, Mr Aegethos.'

He watched her walk away and the back of Laura's neck prickled under the insistent gaze of those dark eyes, but he didn't say anything and she was able to escape unhindered. All the same, she was relieved to close her bedroom door a moment later. She leaned on it in the darkness, her eyes closing and a peculiar weakness in her whole body.

She was not going to be crazy enough to get involved with Domenicos Aegethos, she told herself, trying to shut out the memory of those smouldering dark eyes as they moved over her. Her pulses had leapt and flamed, despite her determination to be unaffected by him. She had never felt a temptation like that before and she did not intend to feel one now.

She scolded herself irritably as she got ready for bed, but sleep was evasive and she lay awake for more than an hour, her mind too disturbed to relax.

She got up late next morning and found Amanda reading a magazine while pop music blared out of the radio. 'Hi, what happened to you?' Amanda asked, lifting an amused face towards her. 'You look like one of the walking dead. Have a good evening, did you?'

'Yes, thank you,' Laura said coolly.

'What did you do?' Amanda giggled. 'Whoops, I take that back. I never asked.'

'Very funny,' Laura said drily. 'I'm going to get some coffee.' She went into the kitchen and made it herself since the housekeeper was not in sight.

When she brought it back Amanda said lazily: 'I'll have a cup.'

'Oh, will you?' Laura poured it and passed her a cup with a wry look. 'How did your dinner with your father go? Did Pierre enjoy it?'

'He was walking on eggshells all evening,' Amanda told her. 'Poor Pierre, he was so polite it hurt.'

Laura glanced at her under her eyelashes. Amanda's voice had had a trace of amused patronage. That didn't sound like blind adoration, she thought. Had Pierre's awe of her father given Amanda a new idea of him? Had she decided he had feet of clay? Laura had a shrewd idea that Amanda was looking for a man who would not be impressed by her father; who would, on the contrary, be more than a match for Domenicos, and a man like that wasn't going to be easy to find.

Mrs Grey appeared half an hour later. She was, she said, lunching out and wouldn't be back until late that afternoon. 'And Domenicos is giving a dinner party here, Amanda, and he would like you and Laura to be here,' she told them, smiling.

'Oh, no!' groaned Amanda. 'Not one of his stuffy parties for some of his business friends? I can't stand it!'

'Please come,' Mrs Grey pleaded, looking at her uncertainly. 'He told me to tell you he expected to see you there.'

'He can expect all he likes,' Amanda said sulkily. 'They bore me stiff, all those bald old guys, talking about interest rates and investment potential. Not my scene.'

Mrs Grey looked at Laura, her eyes begging for help, then she trotted off with Laura's reassuring smile to comfort her.

Amanda caught the smile and eyed Laura warily. 'Don't start,' she said. 'I'm not going.'

'Did I say a word?'

'And don't do that wide-eyed act, because I know you're as cunning as a weasel,' Amanda muttered.

'If you don't want to go, don't,' Laura said mildly. 'I'll explain to your father. The worst he can do is fire me.'

Amanda put her head to one side and viewed her grimly. 'You are the most . . .' She stopped, lost for words.

Laura laughed.

'Give me five minutes and I'll come up with a description that fits,' said Amanda, showing her teeth.

'You could at least keep me company,' Laura said. 'I've had my orders too, remember.'

Amanda gave a deep muffled groan. 'Laura, you have no idea what they're like. Sheer Dullsville on two legs, all of them. Come on, have a heart, let me off.'

'Well, maybe we can think of an excuse your father will swallow,' Laura said slowly. She could well understand why Amanda did not want to be present. She didn't much like the idea herself, and she wondered if they couldn't claim they had tickets for the opera or the theatre for that evening.

'I'll have one of my headaches,' Amanda decided.

'How original!' Laura gave her a dry look.

'Migraine, then,' said Amanda. 'That sounds

much worse. I'll have spots before my eyes and feel sick. That will convince him.'

'You,' said Laura, 'are an optimist.' She did not look forward to offering Domenicos that thin story, but that evening she was able to delay joining the dinner guests until she was sure Domenicos would be too involved with them to have much attention to spare for her or Amanda's absence. She sneaked into the salon unobserved, looking around warily.

The men were all luminaries of the business world, their well-shaven faces courteous, their manners good. The women were elegant and smiled with self-conscious artifice at each other, but under their lowered lashes they gave each other very different glances, dagger-sharp and razor-bright. After a few minutes Laura found herself sitting in a chair with a glass in her hand being sweetly ignored. It didn't bother her. She was enjoying herself, watching, and finding herself apparently invisible made that much easier.

They were competing for Domenicos's attention, she realised. She wasn't quite sure who they were or how well they knew him, but there was no doubt who was the focus of attention and they did not try to hide their eagerness to please him.

It was all very amusing seen from the sidelines. Laura settled down to enjoy the evening.

When Mrs Grey appeared it was without Amanda. She was going to sit down beside Laura when she was drawn into the conversation going on between the other guests, but at a later stage Laura heard her tell her son that Amanda had a headache and was staying in her room.

He glanced sideways at Laura, his dark brows curving. 'She is *in* her room, I suppose?'

'Oh, yes,' Mrs Grey insisted. 'Poor child, she's very pale.'

He frowned. 'Hmm . . .' That long-drawn-out exclamation was familiar to Laura now. Domenicos made that noise when he was doubtful or when he was being sarcastic. She wasn't quite sure which attitude was indicated this time, but his dark eyes held a rueful glint. No doubt he had a pretty shrewd idea why his daughter had absented herself. Laura looked at him and he lifted his wide shoulders in a faint, wry shrug which said a good deal.

They went in to dinner a moment later. The meal was beautifully cooked and the conversation flowed urbanely around the table, accompanied by a good deal of polite laughter at remarks Laura did not find particularly witty but which everyone else apparently did, especially if the light remark came from Domenicos. Oddly, it reminded Laura of Henry. The name-dropping of the guests, the casual mention of famous people they or their friends knew, the outward sophistication and the glitter of money which hung over them all, would have been just up Henry's street. He would have been in his element, Laura thought, smiling to herself.

She caught Domenicos's eye a second later and he signalled curious enquiry about that smile, his brows raised. For a second she had an odd sense of intimacy with him. She felt she could have shared the joke if they had been alone and been certain of an answering, understanding amusement from him. But she looked away, a faint shiver running down her spine. They were a million light years apart, their worlds did not even touch, despite this temporary collision during which she had crashed into his orbit for a while. It could only be dangerous for her to let herself drift into any sort of relationship with him, however tempting it might be.

Out of the corner of her eye she saw one of the women put a pink-nailed hand on his dark sleeve, her head bending towards him. Laura could not hear what she was saying, her voice was low and muffled, but there was nothing muffled about her smile, or the flirtatious look in her eyes.

Laura looked down at her plate, angrily conscious of a nagging ache inside herself. She refused to pursue her own feelings. She did not want to know what had sent that stab of pain through her.

What did it matter to her if Domenicos Aegethos looked into another woman's eyes and smiled in that lazy, amused way? Why should she wonder what the woman was whispering to him? Or why whatever she was saying should bring that mocking enjoyment into his hard face?

From her ringside seat, Laura was being given a very clear idea of the world Domenicos inhabited. She was able to see that sexual magnetism of his in action, watch other women reacting to it, and the sight hardened the feelings inside her. She was not going to let herself slip weakly into looking at him the way those other women were looking. Married or not, they flirted openly, eyeing him with covetous

smiles, and Domenicos flirted right back, teasing
amusement in his eyes. They all had it to a fine art,
Laura thought. It wasn't so much what was said as
how, their eyes saying so much more than their
words, and if their husbands noticed the light flirta-
tions going on they seemed blandly tolerant.
Obviously they either didn't take it seriously or didn't
care one way or the other.

The whole evening underlined for her what her
common sense had already told her. She must not
lose sight of the fact that she did not belong in
Domenicos's world. She must soon go back to the
enclosed world of the hospital, to her friends, her
ordered busy way of life. It all seemed so far away at
the moment. She found it hard to remember that
other world, but she had to make herself remember
it, and recognise that that was where she belonged,
not here.

It was nearly midnight before the guests left. Mrs
Grey vanished soon after eleven, slipping out without
a word during a lively discussion of the political situation in France. Laura saw her go and felt that Mrs
Grey's exit gave her an excuse to follow, but as she
slid out of her chair she caught Domenicos's eye and
he gave her a curt shake of the head, silently ordering
her to stay put.

Laura sank back, frowning, but not quite prepared
to draw the attention of the other guests by attempting to disobey. Domenicos was quite capable of
starting an argument in public, and Laura would
have been covered with embarrassment.

When the guests began to drift off, however, she

seized her opportunity and stole out behind his back as he was saying goodnight. She heard his low voice talking for several minutes as she got ready for bed, then the door closed and she realised the last guests had gone. The apartment was silent. Laura yawned. It had been a dull evening apart from the amusement she had got out of watching these people from another world. A little like a visit to the zoo, she thought. A pity Henry hadn't been there. How he would have loved it.

She got into bed and settled down to go to sleep, but although she lay in the dark for some time willing herself to relax and get to sleep she stayed obstinately awake. It was a situation to which she had been foreign only a short time ago. She had always found it easy to get to sleep in the past. She couldn't think why she found it so hard lately. Presumably, she told herself, it was because she no longer worked so hard and had so much time on her hands during the day.

Sitting up with an impatient murmur, she switched on the bedside lamp and looked for the book she had been reading. It wasn't there. She must have left it somewhere. In the salon? Yes, she thought, remembering. She had had it earlier that day. She thought back to what she had done with it. Pushed it behind a cushion on the sofa?

Sighing, she got out of bed, slipped into her dressing gown and padded barefoot through the dark apartment. The salon was dark, too. Laura switched on the lamp and began turning over the sofa cushions.

'Looking for something?'

The deep voice made her jump and swivel. Domenicos stood in the doorway, his lean body briefly attired in a short black towelling robe, his bare legs damp, his black hair roughly tousled. He held a towel in his hand and had obviously just had a shower.

'Oh! You made me jump!' she groaned.

His dark eyes glinted with amusement. 'Sorry. I heard someone sneaking about and thought it was Amanda doing one of her famous disappearing acts.'

'Oh, I see,' said Laura, smiling nervously, although why she should be feeling slightly weak at the knees she did not know. He walked towards her, the graceful lope of his body riveting her eyes and her throat closed in a sort of mild panic.

'Well, sorry to disturb you,' she said, moving away and making for the door with as much speed as she could without it being too obvious that she was almost running.

He reached out a lazy, confident arm. 'Where are you off to?' he asked in a mocking voice which held the warm purr of a satisfied tiger. 'Not so fast!'

CHAPTER NINE

THE tight circle of his fingers held her wrist too firmly for her to be able to escape. She looked up at him and then wished she hadn't, because there was a very disturbing look in those dark eyes.

'What were you looking for?' he asked.

'A book.'

'Couldn't sleep?'

She shook her head and he laughed softly.

'I thought you slept like a log?'

'I normally do,' she retorted.

'But not tonight?'

Laura looked away, her lashes flickering against her flushed cheeks, and knew he was watching her intently. It worried her even more.

'I wonder why,' Domenicos murmured in that satisfied voice.

'Maybe I'll get to sleep now,' Laura said optimistically, tugging at her imprisoned wrist. 'Excuse me.'

He moved towards the couch without answering and Laura found herself being towed along with him, a protesting captive.

'Mr Aegethos, I want to go back to my room,' she said in a low, husky voice.

He sat down and jerked her down beside him. Laura lifted her head to look at him crossly, and found barbed mockery sparkling in his dark eyes.

'I can't sleep either. Perhaps we both have the same reason for our insomnia,' Domenicos said.

'What's your reason?' she asked, and then knew that that was a mistake. She shouldn't have asked. He had wanted her to and she was playing right into his hands.

'I was thinking,' he said, letting go of her wrist at last but turning to face her, the shift of his long body lazily assured. She found herself staring at the parted lapels of his robe and seeing the brown gleam of his bare skin between them, the strong column of his throat, the few curling black hairs growing on his chest. She did not like the intimacy of this situation. She would have darted away if she had not been sure Domenicos would try to stop her.

'What were you thinking about?' she asked absently, looking away.

'You,' he said softly, and her pulses leapt.

'Oh?' She struggled to sound calm.

'I've never met anyone like you,' he said. 'The more I see of you the more I ask myself if you aren't the exception that proves the rule, the one woman I might actually be able to trust.'

She looked at him warily, moved and touched but still disturbed, and he gave her a wry smile.

'I know you think I'm tough with Amanda, but there are reasons, you know . . .'

'I know,' she said, and his eyes sharpened.

'What do you know?'

She hesitated, frowning.

'My mother told you?' Domenicos asked, and she nodded. 'She gave you her version,' he said tersely.

'Do you want to hear mine?'

'If you want to tell me,' Laura said gently.

'I suppose all of us want to justify ourselves,' Domenicos said in rueful self-derision. 'I was eight when my mother ran off with her lover, and I didn't see her again for years. My uncle was a tough man. He wouldn't let me see her and he made sure I grew up knowing just what she had done to my father and myself.'

Laura moved restlessly, her mouth parting on a protest, and he looked at her, frowning.

'Let me finish. However prettily she may have wrapped it up for you when she told you, the fact is that she dumped me when she went off with that man. She knew what she was doing. She chose her lover and deserted me. I've heard her side of it. She makes my father sound like some sort of monster. Well, he wasn't. He was a reserved man, rather stern, it's true, but he loved her deeply, I know he did. I've got his diaries and it is all there. He fell in love with her on sight and he still loved her the night she ran off with her lover. She broke his heart, and he died a week after she left.'

Laura winced at his expression. 'I can see how it looks from your side, but couldn't you try to see how it looks from hers?' She looked at him pleadingly. 'She just didn't love your father.'

'He was a wonderful man,' Domenicos interrupted, his voice as harsh as his face.

'But love isn't something you can choose to give. It has nothing to do with reason. However wonderful he was, your mother couldn't make herself love him.

She was frightened of him.'

He looked at her restlessly, his mouth taut.

'She says he was an alarming man.' Laura could believe it, looking at his son's strong, angry face. Domenicos in a temper was pretty scary, too.

'He could be very autocratic,' he muttered reluctantly. He looked away, his mouth crooked. 'I remember he used to stand me on a chair so that I was on his eye level and then he would tell me never to forget that life was work—in the last resort nothing else mattered.'

Laura's brows lifted. 'A rather stern idea of life, isn't it?'

'He was like that. He wasn't a man in whose company you could relax. He ran the company like clockwork and he ran his life in the same way.'

'So your mother does have some justification,' she suggested softly. 'You admit he wasn't easy to love.'

'He was her husband,' Domenicos grated, then added harshly: 'And I was her son. She ran out on both of us.'

'Which do you resent the most?'

He gave her a stare, his black brows meeting above that arrogant nose. 'What?'

'I was merely asking,' she said mildly.

'Miss Crawford, I've already discovered one certain thing about you,' Domenicos snapped. 'You never merely do anything: you do everything knowingly. Even the way you move is beautifully controlled. When you pick up a book or a cup you do it with a sort of aware grace which is unforgettable.'

She was too taken aback to say anything, her blue eyes wide in confused surprise.

His face relaxed a little at her expression and he half smiled. 'I thought perhaps it was your training.'

Laura considered that remark with serious interest. 'We're trained to be deft,' she agreed. 'Especially in the operating room. I know nurses who are so quick and smooth at everything they do that before a surgeon has even realised he was going to need some instrument it's being put into his hand.'

'You've worked in the operating room?' he asked, staring at her curiously.

'We train in all the departments before we're allowed to specialise. That way we find out what we like doing, and the hospital finds out what we're good at, where we're most suitable.'

'Isn't it the same thing?' he asked, and she laughed.

'I wish it was—I like operating room work, for instance, and I'm quite good at it, but it seems to have an unfortunate effect on me. I tend to feel sick during major operations.'

'I'm not surprised,' he said. 'So would I.'

'Most people do, but you can't have a surgical nurse who has to keep rushing off to be sick.'

'No,' he agreed drily.

'So I couldn't specialise in that work,' Laura said.

'What did you specialise in?'

She smiled. 'Intensive nursing of accident cases. I work in the unit which specialises in patients who've been involved in serious accidents.'

He stared at her thoughtfully. 'That must be very demanding.'

'But worth while.'

'Especially with your own personal background,' he said quietly, and she nodded. She had forgotten that she had told him all about her family and her reason for taking up nursing.

'You're a dedicated nurse,' he said, still watching her, and she nodded again.

'I like my job.'

'And you're good at it?'

'Very enthusiastic, anyway,' she evaded, smiling.

'How did a level-headed girl like you come to get pneumonia in the first place?'

'You might well ask,' she said wryly. 'Our senior physician was very scathing about my carelessness, but it never occurred to me that I had anything worse than a bad dose of 'flu. It wasn't until I blacked out altogether that my flatmate called the ambulance and I ended up as a patient in my own hospital.' She laughed. 'At least I wasn't in my own ward—that would have been embarrassing. They would never have let me forget that.'

'How ill were you?' Domenicos demanded.

She hesitated then said lightly: 'Oh, well, I survived.'

'My God,' he said in a rough voice. 'That means you were very ill, I suppose?'

'Poorly, as my matron would say,' she agreed, smiling.

'And you look as if one puff of wind would blow you away,' Domenicos said harshly.

'Don't let my looks fool you, Mr Aegethos. I'm stronger than I look.'

'How could you let yourself fall so ill?' he asked, moving restlessly while he stared at her. 'How could you be so stupid?'

'We're all stupid some time or other,' Laura said softly. 'Aren't we?'

His mouth went crooked again and a spark of humour flashed across his eyes. 'Is that meant for me?'

'Don't you think it's time you stopped blaming your mother for something that happened nearly thirty years ago? Do you know that every seven years every cell in your body is renewed? It's a gradual process, but it means that you're physically an entirely different person today compared with the man you were seven years ago. The same applies to your mother. She isn't the woman who ran out on you and your father all those years ago. A lot has happened to both of you since. You're a grown man. Can't you stop punishing her?'

'Punishing her?' he broke out, frowning.

'Don't you?'

'Don't be absurd,' he said shortly. 'Tell me, Miss Crawford, why is it that whenever I try to make headway with you I find myself sidetracked on to other subjects?'

'Do you?' Her blue eyes were evasive and he gave her a long stare, throwing himself backwards, his arms flung over his black head, his body stretching casually, those long bare legs thrust out in front of him.

'You know damned well I do. You're clever with it, I'll grant you. I never quite know what's happening. Somehow the signals change and I'm carefully switched to another line. One minute I'm steaming ahead with a very clear idea of where I'm going. The next I find I'm heading in another direction entirely.'

'What has that to do with your mother?' she asked, and he shook his head warningly at her.

'Ah, no, you aren't sidetracking me again.' He eyed her through his lashes, his mouth curling. 'That solicitor fellow who introduced you to my mother . . .'

'Henry?' Laura smiled.

'Is that his name? Why are you smiling like that?' His dark eyes narrowed. 'Is he a friend—or something more?'

'A friend.'

'Hmm,' he said, and Laura smiled again. 'All right, what's funny now?' he demanded.

'Nothing.'

'You were smiling.'

'Was I? Should I apologise for that?' She gave him a limpid look, amusement in the curve of her mouth, and he laughed under his breath.

'There's another thing about you that's unforgettable.'

'What?' she asked, still amused. 'There's something so charming about flattery, have you ever noticed? It's irresistible, even if you strongly suspect it to be all lies.'

Domenicos laughed and surveyed her closely.

'You've got a sense of humour,' he said. 'That and the graceful way you move make you unusual.' He paused. 'But it's the direct, clear stare of those blue eyes that makes you unique.'

'Thank you,' said Laura, her cheeks pink. 'I'll put it down to the very good wine you had at dinner, shall I? In the morning you'll regret all these overwhelming compliments in case I take them seriously.'

He moved too fast for her to know what was happening. Suddenly his eyes were inches away and his fingers stroked down her flushed cheek. 'Why not?' he asked.

Confused, she frowned. 'Why not what?'

'Take me seriously?'

Warning bells began to clang noisily inside her. She shook her head. 'Oh, no,' she said hurriedly. 'Not me, Mr Aegethos. I'm not crazy.' She would have fled if she could, but he fenced her into the corner of the sofa, his arm barring her escape, his long body looming over her.

A frown drew his brows together. 'What do you mean, not crazy?'

'I'd have to be to start anything with you,' Laura told him, defying him with a nervous, flickering glance. She could feel the muscular pressure of his naked calf against her and she had to look away quickly as her eyes absorbed the smooth tanned skin of his neck and chest when he bent towards her. 'Please, let me go,' she said, her head turned the other way.

He wrenched her chin round and looked into her disturbed eyes. 'But you want to, Laura, don't you?'

She swallowed. 'No.'

His eyes jerked together. 'That's a lie!'

'It is not.' She hoped her voice sounded cool and confident, but she had an uneasy feeling it sounded nothing of the kind. It was very hard to keep her cool when he was so close, those dangerous dark eyes staring into her own.

'I've got a feeling you could drive me mad if I let you,' Domenicos murmured huskily, one thumb flicking along her lower lip. 'I was right about you, wasn't I? You've never been to bed with a man in your life.'

'I'm certainly not going to bed with you,' Laura told him. 'I'm flattered by the proposition, but no, thank you, Mr Aegethos.'

'I haven't put a proposition yet,' he pointed out, pushing back a wandering strand of silky blonde hair, and her nerve ends tingled as his hand curved round her cheek.

'Then don't bother, because the answer is no.'

'Is it?' He bent forward and his mouth softly slid down the side of her throat and Laura's breath stopped for a second.

'Don't!' she almost wailed. 'I don't like it.'

She heard his muffled laughter as he explored the tender skin behind her ear, pushing back her tumbling hair to expose it before he moved his mouth along the rounded curve of her cheek until he was kissing the soft warm flesh under her chin. Laura did not want to enjoy it. She wanted to push him away, reject the delicate seduction before it became really disturbing, but another part of her mind loved it, yearned to submit without protest, and she was so occupied in the internal struggle between her common sense and her emotions that Domenicos had captured her mouth before she woke up to how far he had got.

The fierce pressure of his mouth surprised her lips into parting, trembling into an answering passion. Her hands went up to catch his black head, hold it possessively, her fingers running into his thick smooth hair, her body restless and quivering as he pressed down against her. His hand slid inside her dressing gown and she felt it warmly caress her breast. Desire drowned the last remnant of her common sense. She groaned, one hand sliding down the side of his neck and between the parted lapels, to find the warm brown skin, the deep rapid beat of his heart racing against her own.

Domenicos lifted his head and looked passionately at her. 'Is the answer still no, Laura?'

Eyes half closed, she abandoned everything. She knew she would die of frustration if he stopped now. Let tomorrow look after itself. If she was going to get hurt, that was just too bad. She would have to bear it, but she knew she couldn't bear it if she rejected the feverish drag of desire which Domenicos had started inside her.

'Yes or no?' he whispered.

Laura's hand stroked down the taut pathway of his body, her heart racing. 'Yes,' she moaned, eyes closed.

He kissed her hard. 'I think I'm in love with you,' he said huskily, and Laura's eyes slowly fluttered open.

'What?' She couldn't believe her ears.

He was flushed and his mouth was crooked. 'I haven't been in love since I was very young,' he said wryly. 'My wife and I were in love, but somehow it all went wrong. I didn't so much fall out of love as wake up one day and realise to my shock that I had never been in love with her at all. I'd been in love with love, but I hadn't really known my wife at all. Lina wasn't the woman I had thought she was, that was all. The magic went out of it. She knew, of course. How could she avoid knowing?' His sigh was bitter. 'That was why she started flirting with someone else, of course. She thought if she made me jealous I'd fall in love again. But it didn't work.'

Poor woman, Laura thought. What a painful tangle! Domenicos looked down at her and gave another long sigh.

'It was all my fault but I didn't have the grace to admit as much to her. I was angry at the time. I felt she had publicly humiliated me by having an affair with someone else.' He grimaced. 'I was a selfish young swine.'

'I won't argue with you,' Laura said gently.

He half laughed. 'No, I can read what you think in your eyes. Your eyes show everything, do you know that?'

'I don't like the sound of that.'

He smiled. 'I do. That's one of the reasons I've fallen in love with you, those beautiful big blue eyes. I didn't think I'd ever fall in love again. After my marriage broke up I told myself that love was all an illusion, a charade, a confidence trick. There was no such thing. There was just sexual attraction, chemistry, the physical need for satisfaction, and no one woman mattered more than any other. So why bother to get married again?'

'It makes sense—of a sort, I suppose,' Laura admitted.

'And then I met you,' he murmured, smiling. 'You looked very delicate and feminine. You had the loveliest eyes I'd ever seen and your smile was dazzling, but I hadn't known you two minutes when I began to think you were the most obstinate, opinionated woman I'd ever met. That day in my office—you laid into me on the subject of Amanda without hesitation. I was very annoyed with you, but I kept remembering the way your blue eyes smiled once or twice, and I must admit that that was why I chose to come to Paris.'

Laura eyed him thoughtfully. 'You chose to come?'

'I made an excuse,' he said unashamedly. 'It wasn't necessary for me to come here to do this negotiating. It could have been done by one of my executives. George could have done it. But I decided I'd be interested in getting another look at you.'

'You came here with the set intention of seducing me!' Laura accused, staring at him in incredulity.

He grinned. 'I plead guilty.'

'Good lord,' she said. 'What a fiend you are!'

That pleased him. 'Sorry,' he said, his eyes amused.

'And I never guessed,' she murmured, her brow wrinkling.

'I'm more adroit than to make it obvious,' Domenicos told her.

'You certainly don't believe in wasting time, though, do you?' she asked. 'The night you arrived . . .'

'Yes, I was tempted by finding you alone here,' he admitted. 'You looked very sexy in that black kaftan.'

'Thank you.'

He laughed. 'Don't look at me like that.'

'I've a good mind to hit you with something!' Laura exclaimed. 'If I'd had any idea!'

'You would have been even more difficult to catch,' he mocked, watching her.

She looked at him through half-lowered lashes. 'You haven't caught me yet.'

'Oh, yes,' he said softly. 'You are well and truly caught, Miss Crawford.'

A little shiver ran down her spine and she frowned. 'I don't know that I like the sound of this carefully followed plan.' She did not like the sound of it at all.

'The plan went out of the window almost at once,' he said. 'When you talked to me that night about your family, the car crash, your reason for becoming a nurse. While I was listening I was watching you, and although I still thought you very sexy, very enticing, I began to see you in a very different light. The more I got to know you the more I liked you. It's one thing to plan to seduce a pretty girl you've only met once. Most girls are flattered by ideas like that. After all, I'd gone to the trouble of following you to Paris. Isn't that flattering?'

'Not very,' Laura said drily. 'It comes in the category of expensive hobbies, I'd say.'

He laughed. 'What a biting little tongue you've got! Anyway, I didn't pursue my plan.'

'You didn't?' She wasn't quite ready to believe that.

Domenicos shook his head. 'I may be what you call a fiend, but I couldn't quite go ahead with a coldblooded plan to seduce a girl I was beginning to like very much.'

Laura surveyed him warily. 'What was going on just now? I distinctly recall a proposition being made.'

'And accepted,' he mocked, his eyes wicked.

She flushed. 'Very well, and accepted,' she admitted.

'I wasn't actually making a proposition,' he said, kissing her lightly. 'I was sort of asking you to marry me.'

Her heart turned over inside her chest with a disturbing flop. 'Sort of?' she asked shakily.

Domenicos shrugged, his face rather flushed, his eyes restless. 'I couldn't quite get the words out. I felt rather stupid, to tell you the truth. I thought I might get my point over in a roundabout way, lead up to it gradually, and find out on the way whether or not you felt the same way.' He glanced at her and away again, his mouth twisting. 'Do you?'

Laura put a hand against his cheek and turned his head towards her gently. Looking into his dark eyes, she said: 'Yes.'

A smile broke on his face. 'Laura,' he said deeply.

'I love you,' she said. 'I knew it was for real tonight at dinner when you looked at me.'

'When you were smiling to yourself? What was that about?'

'I was thinking about Henry,' she said.

Domenicos frowned. 'Henry makes you smile?' He didn't like the sound of that, she saw, and she said with amusement: 'If you knew him it would have made you smile.' Her fingers stroked along his chin. 'I wanted to tell you, share it with you, and that was when I realised how deep it was, the way I felt. Wanting to share jokes is part of love.'

'Love isn't what I thought it was,' he said.

'It never is,' Laura told him. 'That's the thing about love—you never know what to expect.'

'Love's like Christmas,' Domenicos murmured, smiling to himself. 'Full of surprises. I can't wait to unwrap my present.'

Pink stole up into her face at the mockery of his glance. 'Domenicos!' she scolded, pretending to be deeply shocked. 'And I was beginning to believe you loved me for my mind alone . . .'

'That, too,' he said. 'But luckily your mind comes in a most delightful package . . .'

His dark head bent towards her and Laura ran both arms around his neck and lifted her face for his kiss.

A WORD ABOUT THE AUTHOR

harlotte Lamb was born and raised in London's East
nd. To this day she remains at heart an unswerving
ondoner, although for the past several years she has lived
n the rain-swept Isle of Man in the Irish Sea. Charlotte
kens the Isle of Man to the setting of Emily Brontë's
'uthering Heights and says that all one can see for miles
round are "sheep and heather-covered moors."

Charlotte began writing romances in 1970. Her very
rst attempt was accepted by Mills & Boon, and she has
ever looked back.

Since those earlier days, she has become amazingly
rolific. Always a fast typist, she can now create and
ommit to paper at least one novel a month! "I love to
rite, and it comes easily to me," she explains. "My
ooks practically write themselves."

The fact that Charlotte has been married now for more
han two decades, and is the devoted mother of five
hildren ranging in age from seven to twenty, immediately
rings to mind the question: where does she find the time
accomplish all her excellent writing? "I have a very
ood housekeeper," she says with a smile . . . as if that
xplains everything!